The messy bed drew Cade's attention.

Summer had never been a neat freak, but the disheveled covers looked as if they'd hosted a wrestling match.

He licked his lips and met Lori's glassy eyes for a split second. Then he charged out of the room, calling his sister's name. He dipped his head into the kitchen, scanning the dirty dishes in the sink... and a broken glass on the floor.

"Her car's gone. Maybe she left a mess and took off before she could pick up." Before she could pick up a broken glass on the kitchen floor?

Lori didn't reassure him. In fact, she said nothing at all as she crouched beside the front door, her back to him, her shoulders stiff.

Cade wiped the back of his hand across his mouth. "What's wrong?"

She twisted her head over her shoulder and whispered, "I found a bloody fingerprint."

CANYON CRIME SCENE

———

CAROL ERICSON

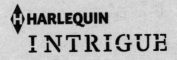

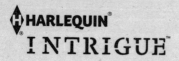

ISBN-13: 978-1-335-58203-4

Canyon Crime Scene

Copyright © 2022 by Carol Ericson

Recycling programs
for this product may
not exist in your area.

Harlequin Enterprises ULC
22 Adelaide St. West, 41st Floor
Toronto, Ontario M5H 4E3, Canada
www.Harlequin.com

Printed in U.S.A.

Carol Ericson is a bestselling, award-winning author of more than forty books. She has an eerie fascination for true-crime stories, a love of film noir and a weakness for reality TV, all of which fuel her imagination to create her own tales of murder, mayhem and mystery. To find out more about Carol and her current projects, please visit her website at www.carolericson.com, "where romance flirts with danger."

Visit the Author Profile page at Harlequin.com.

CAST OF CHARACTERS

Cade Larson—This New Yorker returns to his native LA to visit his troubled younger sister, but she goes missing and he reconnects with his former love to track her down in a perilous game of cat and mouse.

Lori Del Valle—A fingerprint tech for the LAPD, she puts herself in danger to help her high school sweetheart locate his missing sister...and may end up finding herself in the process.

Summer Larson—Cade's sister has always had a talent for getting into trouble, but this time she may not be able to use her family's money and influence to get out of it.

Trey Ferrar—His best friend goes missing about the same time as Summer, but he knows a dangerous secret that might save them even while it puts a target on his back.

Wade Dufrain—A self-help guru, he runs an exclusive recovery center for women but employs some questionable treatment methods.

Danny Del Valle—Lori's brother is doing time for murdering his girlfriend, but Lori hasn't given up searching for the one fingerprint that could clear him.

Chapter One

The gates to the California Correctional Institution closed behind her, and Lori stepped on the gas as she smeared a tear across her cheek with the back of her hand. The tears always came later. She never gave in to them while sitting across from Danny.

She hadn't been able to bring her brother any good news this time as he endured his sixth year behind bars for a crime he didn't commit. As if Danny would've killed his girlfriend. He'd loved Elena more than anything in the world.

He'd loved her...passionately. The little voice whispered in her ear, "too passionately?" She brushed away the words along with another tear making its way down her face.

That's what the DA had insisted. Danny had killed Elena in a fit of passion. That's why the DA's office had charged him with manslaughter instead of first- or even second-degree murder. That and Danny's confession.

He'd only pleaded guilty to get the deal. Danny

had assured her he hadn't done it and she believed him...because of the fingerprint.

She flexed her hands on the steering wheel, her palms sweaty, as she accelerated onto the freeway that would take her back to LA. The police had found a fingerprint at Elena's murder scene that they couldn't identify. They never did ID it but hadn't tried too hard after Danny confessed to the murder.

And Lori had been looking for the owner of that print ever since. After college, she'd been heading for a career in forensics anyway, but the mystery of that print had led her to fingerprint analysis and a career as a fingerprint tech with the LAPD.

She'd just finished a stint on a serial killer task force where she'd made a couple of big contributions and had gotten on the radar of the new captain at the Northeast Division. She worked hard and loved her job, but her brother's case always loomed in the background. She compared every print she came across in her line of work to the one at Elena's crime scene.

Her former boss, Clive Stewart, had caught on to what she was doing, but then Clive had turned out to be the infamous serial killer The Player and now he was dead, so she didn't have to worry about him. The fact that the LAPD had a serial killer working on its forensics team for over twenty years had been a source of embarrassment for the department and Chief Sterling, and they had cracked down on policy and procedure—but there was always a way around that. She should know. She'd learned it from a master—not that her workarounds were remotely in the same league as Clive's. She'd never liked the guy. She'd grown up around enough shady characters to smell one out across the lab from her.

As she left the snow-capped peaks of the Tehachapi Mountains in her rearview, her phone rang. She glanced at the display before putting her cell on Speaker.

"Hola, Mama."

"Did you see him?"

"Just left."

"How does he look? Is he eating right?"

"He looked fine." Except for the prison tat on his neck that he'd acquired since the last time she'd visited. Did he think that was going to help him land a job when he got out, even if she could prove his innocence?

Her mother released an audible, soggy breath. "Is he still too skinny? Tell me, *mija.*"

Lori squeezed her eyes closed for a second, seeing Danny's slim frame and concave chest. "He's the same, Mama."

Her mother paused. "He still says he's innocent?"

"He doesn't have to say that to me." Lori's temples throbbed. "I believe him."

"Okay. It's okay, *mija.* I know you do." Her mother's voice soothed like a pat on the head.

Then she started talking about her other children—the ones that mattered—Lori's older brother, Raymund, who was a police officer in San Antonio, and her older sister, Rita, who lived in the Netherlands with her husband, who worked at the State Department.

They'd all given up on Danny when he'd confessed to Elena's murder, and Mom had moved back to Mexico to take care of Abuela, although the old lady didn't really need the help. Dad would've stood by his son, but he'd died two years before Danny's arrest.

That left Lori to fight for him, although some days, like today, Danny didn't seem to want the help.

Lori let Mom ramble on for several miles. What else did she have to occupy her time? The landscape that rolled past her window presented a stark view. The snow from the mountains that had made it down to this elevation had all melted away with the coming spring, and a brown, drab color scheme painted the rolling hills waiting for the greenery of new growth.

Southern California had suffered a hot, dry summer the year before and several wildfires had blasted the region. Those splashes of green in this area might be a long time coming.

She blinked when she heard her mother say her name. "Lori?"

"I'm sorry—what did you say?"

Mom sighed. "I asked if you were still doing okay after finding out your boss was a killer."

"I told you, Mama. It didn't affect me. I wasn't in any danger from Clive."

Her mother tutted. "You always told me he didn't like you."

"He didn't, but he didn't want to kill me. He saw me as a threat to his job."

"*Dios mio.* To be that close to a killer."

"Definitely a creep." Lori slowed down when she spotted a familiar fast-food sign on the side of the road. "Hey, Mom. I'm going to pull in to get something to drink for the rest of the ride home. I'll call you later, and give my love to Abuelita."

Fifteen minutes later with a drink in her cup holder and the radio blasting '80s music, Lori hopped back on the freeway to LA. She'd planned her visit to Danny at the beginning of family time so she'd make it home before nightfall.

As she cruised on the highway, her phone buzzed and she tapped to answer it.

Her boss's voice boomed through the car. "Hey, Lori. Are you anywhere near the station? Please tell me you're not in Big Bear catching the end of the ski season or camped out poolside in Palm Springs getting a jump start on your tan."

"I wish." She gazed out her windshield at the barren hillsides as she swooped down into the Los Angeles basin. "Why would I be in either of those places?"

"Because two of your coworkers are, and I need someone to process prints at a possible crime scene in Hollywood."

Her heart skipped a beat, just as it always did at the mention of a crime scene. "Possible?"

"A guy came into the Northeast Division yesterday to report his friend missing. The desk sergeant told him to come back when it had been forty-eight hours. The same guy called in today to tell us he'd broken into his friend's house and found a mess and some blood. Now we have a possible crime scene."

Glancing at the clock on the dashboard, she said, "I'm driving back into town, but I'm about forty minutes from the station. I'll drop by and get my kit and head over to the crime scene."

Doug said, "*Possible* crime scene."

"Right." She ended the call and put pressure on the accelerator.

She'd lied to Doug. More than an hour stretched between her and the station, but a girl had to do what a girl had to do to stay on top of her game.

By the time Lori rolled up to the neat stucco house in Hollywood, her bag of tricks slung over her shoulder, LAPD Detective Jane Falco was in the front yard directing traffic.

As Lori jogged across the street to join the gaggle of CSIs grouped around Detective Falco awaiting orders, she eyed the detective's pantsuit and sleek ponytail, wishing she'd had time to change out of her jeans and sneakers before arriving. Visiting day at the correctional institution didn't demand professional attire.

She sidled up to the edge of the circle, brushing her bangs from her eyes.

Detective Falco pinned her with a gaze and raised her eyebrows. "Del Valle, fingerprints?"

"Yes, ma'am." Lori's heart didn't pitter-patter too much at the recognition. After all, she'd worked side by side with a serial killer and hadn't noticed a thing—until the end. Maybe the detective knew her name because she'd been clueless, not because she'd finally reported her boss for odd behavior.

Falco nodded. "I was just saying, the missing woman's friend tried to make a report yesterday, after checking area hospitals, but Courtney had just skipped a lunch date and the friend couldn't reach her. Knowing he had to wait another twenty-four hours before he could report her missing, he took matters into his own hands today and broke into her house through a back window. He noticed some disturbance and blood in the bedroom and called us."

Lori asked, "Do we have the friend's prints on file to rule them out?"

"I'm going to leave that to you, Del Valle. Do it at the station. The friend—" Falco checked her notes "—Trey Ferrar, is coming in for a formal interview. You can take his prints there."

Detective Falco gave them a few more instructions before turning toward the house next door to Courtney's to start her canvassing of the neighborhood. The department had just transferred Detective Falco to the Northeast Division and the gossip already had her pegged as a by-the-book stickler. Lori didn't mind as long as the detective stayed out of her business.

Lori hitched the bag onto her shoulder and followed the other CSIs into the house. They already knew Trey had broken in through the back window, so she'd start there and get his prints.

The break-in point turned out to be a window over the sink in the kitchen. Trey had jimmied the sliding glass out of its tracks and lifted it free from the frame. He'd left a shoe print in the sink as he climbed into the house, knocking a glass to the floor on his way. Lori dusted the window frame and the counter and lifted both finger and palm prints, as he probably braced himself before he jumped to the floor.

She didn't bother with the rest of the kitchen, as she had no interest in random visitors to Courtney's house. She had to hit the areas where smears of blood had been found, specifically Courtney's bedroom and the door leading to the garage.

Courtney's car was also missing and who was to say the young woman didn't cut herself and drive to the emergency room? Except her friend hadn't found a record of her at any hospital emergency room in the area, and her car hadn't been located.

Lori crouched down to study the blood smears and sucked in a breath. She called out to anyone within shouting distance. "I found a patent print in the blood on the garage door."

Lori hadn't even heard Detective Falco return to

the house, but she hovered over her shoulder now and said, "Good job, Del Valle."

"Ah, you can call me Lori, and Clive Stewart may have been a serial killer but he taught me well." She twisted around to retrieve a tool from her bag, and her gaze collided with Detective Falco's piercing green eyes.

"That's not funny, Del Valle."

"No, ma'am." Lori returned to her task, rolling her eyes. Falco had better learn to lighten up if she planned to work with Jake McAllister and Billy Crouch, the two hotshot detectives at the Northeast Division who played fast and loose and still managed to solve four copycat killer cases and nail the original, her boss, Clive Stewart.

When she finished taking the prints from the house, with the prerogative to return if she needed more, Lori packed up her tools and drove back to the station. There, she'd take Trey's prints and eliminate his and Courtney's from the one she took at the house. She hoped neither of theirs matched the patent print left in the blood. She didn't even know whose blood that was yet, but she'd bet on it being Courtney's.

When she got back to the station, she noticed Trey Ferrar already sitting at a desk, his head in his hands. Lori hesitated and raised her eyebrows at Detective Falco across the room, who gave her a slight nod.

Lori approached Trey and cleared her throat.

The young man's head jerked up, and he swiped a hand across his eyes.

"Hi, Trey, my name's Lori Del Valle, and I'm going to take your fingerprints just so we can rule them out at Courtney's house. Is that all right?" Not that Trey had a choice, but it sounded nicer to ask.

He gave her a jerky nod and said, "Here?"

"I'll take you to the machine." She waved her hand over her shoulder. "We don't have to roll prints these days. We can do them electronically."

He rose to his feet and followed her to a small room where they handled the prints. While she instructed him where to put his fingers, Lori peppered him with questions. "Why did you suspect something wrong when Courtney didn't show up for lunch?"

"Court's always on time and she never misses a date—not with me, anyway." He flicked a black curl from his eyes.

"Are you two...dating?"

Trey's nostrils flared. "I'm not into girls. Court's my BFF. We're each other's confidantes."

"Has she confided anything to you recently about going away or meeting someone new or being scared?"

"She's been..."

"Are you finished in here?"

Lori glanced up at Falco filling the door, her head cocked to one side. What Courtney had been doing, Lori would never know now.

"Yep, all done." Falco must be great at interrogations. She could make you feel guilty with one look from those cat eyes, but Lori didn't feel an ounce of embarrassment for questioning Trey. Maybe he'd let something slip that he wouldn't tell a detective.

She ushered Trey out of the room and went to the CSI lab. Not all LAPD divisions had their own CSI labs, but the Northeast Division had been remodeled recently and the station had gotten a fancy one. The lab handled work for smaller LAPD divisions, and she could count on a steady stream of techs in and out of the room during the week. Sundays tended to be slower, so she and the team that had worked Courtney's house today had the place to themselves.

Lori processed the prints from the house, labeling both Courtney's and Trey's prints for comparison. Her heart thumped a little faster when she realized the print in the blood didn't match either of theirs. Maybe Courtney's kidnapper had been sloppy.

She put together an impression of the print to email to IAFIS but as this was still a missing person and not a homicide, she didn't expect speedy results. She'd send out the email tomorrow morning.

She waved to the remaining tech in the lab, as she left and walked down the hallway. She passed the conference room that had doubled as the Copycat Player task force room, now back to its sedate oval table and chairs, the electricity gone, ready to host the next meeting of the brass on finance or citizen complaints.

She jogged downstairs to the reception area, a

loud, irate, totally male voice disrupting the typical somnolence of a Sunday evening. She hid a smirk as the man looming over the front-desk sergeant pounded his fist on the counter.

His voice rose. "I don't care if it hasn't been forty-eight hours. I know my sister."

Not just the words but the set of the man's broad shoulders and the sweep of his dark blond hair gave Lori pause, and she stumbled to a stop and turned toward the commotion.

Sergeant Cerda glanced at her past the irate citizen and lifted one eyebrow.

The imposing figure turned, and Lori pressed her hand against her chest as she met the smoldering blue gaze of the man who'd stolen her heart.

She'd repaid him for that theft by deceiving him in the worst possible way.

Chapter Two

His blood pressure spiking, Cade Larson spun around mid-rant when he noticed the desk sergeant making faces at someone behind him. His eyes narrowed as he took in the attractive brunette gawping at him from across the room.

A warm flush crawled up his chest and he unclenched his fists. He probably was making an ass of himself, acting like his entitled father, but Summer was worth it.

When the woman finally picked up her jaw from the floor, she took a tentative step toward him and said, "Cade?"

The heat, which had been subsiding, rushed back, engulfing his face.

Cade swallowed hard as his gaze skimmed over Loretta Del Valle's curvy body, snug in a pair of jeans, her hand held up in a tentative wave as if uncertain if he'd remember her. Some nights he'd found her hard to forget.

He reversed his scowl into the smile that could

charm an agreement and a signature from the most skeptical of business associates. "What are you doing at a police station, Lori?"

He clenched his teeth behind the smile. Dumb question. This could have something to do with her brother Danny.

She tucked a strand of chocolate-brown hair behind one ear. "I work here. What's your excuse?"

"Are you a cop?" He snapped his fingers. "No, forensics or something, right?"

Her dark eyes widened for a second before she strode across the floor toward him, her sneakers squeaking on the linoleum. She thrust out her hand. "Good to see you, Cade, and it's fingerprints."

He took her hand, the professional gesture throwing cold water on his daydreams, her warm, soft skin firing them up again. "That's right. Fingerprints."

She practically snatched her hand from his and tucked it behind her back as if afraid he'd take it again. "Now that my presence here at the Northeast Division is explained, it's your turn. I thought you lived in…somewhere else."

Cade's heart stuttered in his chest. She knew he lived in New York? He glanced back at the officer behind the counter, whose eyes were glued to a computer screen, while the tilt of his head indicated he'd heard every word exchanged between him and Lori.

"I, uh…" Cade dipped his head, remembering the way he'd been haranguing the officer when Lori happened by. He scooped in a deep breath. "I came out to LA to see my sister, and now she's missing."

Lori gasped and grabbed his arm, squeezing it. "Summer?"

"Yeah, Summer." Cade had two sisters—one older and one younger—but Lori figured right away that it was his younger sister in trouble and not his perfect older sister, Sarah. He and Lori had bonded in high school over the problems of their siblings, except his family had the money to buy Summer out of trouble and Danny had wound up in prison—not that Summer had ever murdered anyone...not that he knew of, anyway.

"I'm so sorry." She slid a glance at the uniform not even pretending not to listen anymore. "How long has she been missing?"

"Since about seven o'clock last night." He gripped the edge of the counter, his anxiety taking hold of him again. "She was supposed to meet me for dinner in Santa Monica."

"Santa Monica? What are you doing at this station?"

"She lives up this way. My hotel is in Santa Monica, and she wanted to go to a place near the pier—only she never showed up."

Lori gestured toward the officer. "That's why the police can't take a report yet. An adult has to be missing for forty-eight hours unless there are signs of foul play."

Cade smacked his palm against his forehead.

Hunching over the counter, he said, "I'm sorry for yelling, Sergeant Cerda. I'm worried about my sister."

"I understand, Mr. Larson. If you still haven't located her in the next twenty-four hours, come back and I'll send you right up to a detective."

"Thanks, Gary." Lori tapped on the counter. "I—I can be here tomorrow when you come back, Cade. Just, you know…"

"That would be great, Lori." He stepped away from the counter, and steered Lori away with a hand on the small of her back. "But what's this tomorrow stuff? Are you free now for a drink or a coffee?"

The hand clutching the strap of her bag tightened, but it didn't sport a wedding ring on her finger. Didn't mean she didn't have a man waiting for her at home. Lucky bastard.

"I'm sorry. That was a dumb idea. Y-you're probably busy." And just like that, Lori Del Valle had managed to turn him into a stuttering high school jock again.

She scooted a little farther from the reception area and lowered her voice. "Actually, I'm not busy. I was just going to head home and eat something. I had to come right into work after visiting Danny today, and I'm starving."

He grinned like an idiot. "Perfect—I mean, not that you had to see Danny behind bars or that you're starving or…"

She cut off his rambling with a hand to his chest. "I know what you mean. Do you have a rental car?"

"How else am I supposed to get around LA? Where's your place?" His face warmed. "So we don't go someplace out of the way."

She withdrew her hand from his shirtfront and stuck it in the pocket of her jacket. "I'm not too far from Santa Monica. I'm currently staying in a house in Venice—on the canals."

He raised his eyebrows. "Nice spot."

"Being a fingerprint tech doesn't pay that well. I'm renting the house from a friend at an extremely reduced rate. She insisted. Gave me some story about not being able to rent it out after what happened there."

"What happened there?"

"A murder." She dug her keys out of her purse and waved them in the air. "Why don't we head back to Santa Monica, park in the structure on Third and find a place to eat around there?"

Cade wanted to ask if her house was safe. He wanted to ask her if she had a boyfriend. He wanted to ask her a million questions, but he didn't want to break this spell right now.

Instead of giving her the third degree, he said, "That sounds good. I'll follow you."

They walked out to the parking lot together, and she jerked her thumb at a black SUV. "This is me. Traffic shouldn't be too bad right now, but in case you lose me I can give you my number."

He pulled his phone from his pocket. "Give me your number now, and I'll call you so I have it."

He tapped in her number, she answered and he hung up. "Got it. See you in a few."

He followed her onto the freeway and kept close on her tail. His familiarity with the city matched hers, as they'd both grown up in LA—she on the east side of LA and he in Malibu. They'd attended the same private high school. Lori had gotten a scholarship but fit in as seamlessly as he did. Without the money and the legacy connections, Lori had used her brains and her warmth to adapt to the rich-kid vibe at Brentwood Prep. Despite Lori's good grades and popularity, his parents didn't approve of their relationship. They thought her brother Danny would have a bad influence on her, never acknowledging that they had a troubled daughter of their own.

Cade's hands involuntarily squeezed the steering wheel of his rental. Why would Summer take off without telling him? She hadn't mentioned a boyfriend, but then he didn't know any of her friends. He didn't even know if she had a job. Dad sent her money like clockwork from Japan, where he and Mom had been the past few years, setting up a new business venture.

Dad had agreed to support her financially as long as she stayed in college, but Summer didn't have to send proof of her enrollment. Dad should've known that without accountability, Summer would do what she wanted. She always had, but Mom and

Dad firmly ascribed to the adage of *out of sight, out of mind* and were comfortable with the arrangement.

But he wasn't. He'd decided to take a few weeks away from his business and come out to LA to get Summer back on track. Maybe his sister was running away from him. Maybe Sergeant Cerda was right—adults took off all the time without telling people, and they had the right to do so…especially people like Summer. She most likely didn't have a job, wasn't in school, had disposable income…and liked to party, which was a benign way of saying she was a drug addict.

Cade had been able to stay behind Lori and followed her off the freeway and into one of the parking structures that handled the vehicles for the outdoor Third Street Promenade. The area still drew the crowds, even on a Sunday night, but he had no trouble nabbing a parking spot on the same aisle as Lori.

She waited for him by the stairs of the garage and eyed him up and down as he approached her. "Good, you have a coat. On the way over here, I developed a sudden craving for some fresh seafood. Do you want to catch a bite at the fish market on the pier and eat at the tables outside?"

He'd had something a little more formal in mind, but Lori usually went for adventurous over formal. "Whatever you like. I'm the one who strong-armed you into this date."

She wrinkled her nose. "It's not really a date, just two old friends catching up."

Lori seemed determined to put some space between them, or at least to downplay their previous relationship, and he'd honor that. It meant no reliving those steamy nights in the backseat of his car or in a sleeping bag at the beach when they couldn't keep their hands off each other. His gaze wandered to her backside, cupped in a pair of tight jeans, swaying in rhythmic motion as she preceded him down the stairs. Not even the stench of urine that permeated the stairwell could blot out her sweet smell. She must use the same perfume or lotion she'd used as a teen. The smell had haunted him and triggered thoughts of a youthful first love for nine years. He'd even broken off an engagement because the woman didn't smell right. He'd better not admit that to this no-nonsense, professional woman in front of him.

At the fish market, they both ordered grilled mahi, Cajun style, with French fries and coleslaw, and carried their paper plates to the picnic tables that afforded them a view of the tourists clogging the wooden pier in search of souvenirs and food.

Cade allowed Lori a minute to squeeze lemon on her fish, and take a bite of coleslaw and a sip of her soda, before he started. "Married? Children?"

Lori coughed on her drink, and her eyes watered. "No and no. You?"

He tried to contain his sigh of relief, which made it out his nose anyway and ended in a snort. "Almost and no."

She dropped her little plastic fork and dove beneath the table to retrieve it. Her muffled voice asked, "You almost had a child or you were almost married?"

"I answered in order." He cocked his head at her as she popped up, her face flushed. "You're going to use that fork?"

"Five-second rule." She polished the tines of the fork with a napkin. "You almost got married? You didn't strand anyone at the altar, did you?"

"Me?" He aimed his own fork at his chest. "I wouldn't do something like that, but I was the one who ended things. Just didn't seem…right. How about you? Boyfriend? Any near misses?"

He held his breath as she toyed with her fish.

"A few boyfriends here and there. Ended a relationship about six months ago over work. It hadn't lasted long—nothing much has. Like you said, just didn't seem…right."

Did the guy have the wrong smell? He coughed. "Tell me about the house in Venice. A murder, really?"

Lori planted her elbows on the table, her hesitation gone now that the conversation had veered away from the personal. "You heard about the Copycat Player killings, right?"

"I did." His hand carrying his cup to his mouth jerked and the ice rattled. "Tell me one of the victims did not live in that house."

"No, it belonged to a retired LAPD detective, the one who missed the original Player twenty years ago.

The Player murdered the detective in the house. I know Detective Quinn's heir, and she asked me to stay in the house. I think she's just doing me a favor. My landlord kicked me out of the duplex I was renting because she wanted her son to live there. Kyra knew I was looking for a place and offered me the house for nothing close to what she could get for rent."

"Some favor." He dragged a fry through some ketchup. "Is it safe, this house in Venice?"

"Of course. The Player is dead and gone."

He dropped the French fry, bleeding red. "When my sister didn't show up last night at the restaurant and then didn't answer my calls, that's what I thought about—all those women The Player and his copycats killed."

Lori shifted her hand across the table, her fingers inches from his, almost touching him. "I'm sure that's not what's going on here. Does Summer have a boyfriend?"

"Not that I know of." He ran a hand through his hair, the ends curling from the damp ocean air. "I haven't been a good brother. I know nothing about her life, but I kind of hoped to remedy that with this trip."

"From what I remember about Summer, she's independent that way."

His sharp laugh startled the seagull on the alert for scraps of food, and it flapped away to the next table. "That's one way of putting it."

Lori asked, "Where does she live? Have you tried showing up on her doorstep?"

"She lives in Los Feliz. I'd just been to her place before I came to the station to file a missing persons report." He spread his hands. "Lights on, nobody answered the door, nobody home."

Lori drummed her fingers on the table. "I suppose you don't have a key to her place."

"Key?" He raised his eyebrows. "I'm lucky I got the address out of her."

Lori grabbed her cup and puckered her lips around the straw, her dark eyes glimmering as she stared over his shoulder.

"What are you thinking?" He hunched forward, splaying his hands on either side of her plate. "That's the same look you always got just before daring me to do some ridiculous stunt."

"Just came from a situation like yours." She held up one finger as he opened his mouth. "This guy tried to report his friend missing, but just like Summer his friend hadn't been gone for forty-eight hours yet. He took matters into his own hands and broke into the friend's place. There were signs of a struggle, some blood stains and poof—" she snapped her fingers "—just like that, the police came out to investigate. Now they have probable cause and not just a worried friend...or brother."

Cade narrowed his eyes. "Are you suggesting I break into my sister's place?"

She stuffed a fry in her mouth and waved her

hands as she chewed. "I'm not *suggesting* anything. I'm just telling you what got the attention of the police."

"Will you go with me?"

Her head jerked up. "Me? You want me to go with you to break into your sister's place?"

"You always were my favorite partner in crime." He brushed his thumb across the back of her hand. "It might help me find out where she is. Maybe I don't need to file a report at all. She lives alone, and it's not as if Summer's going to press charges against me for breaking into her home. The cops didn't charge that guy for breaking into his friend's house, right?"

"What are we talking about here? Apartment? House? Los Feliz is kind of upscale, trendy."

"My parents wouldn't relegate Summer to an apartment. She lives in a house, definitely near the trendy part of Los Feliz."

"I'm in."

And just like that, he had Lori Del Valle on his side again. He smothered his smile with a hand. Didn't want to come off as smug or triumphant, although he did feel like he'd just won an award.

Crumpling his napkin, he said, "Let's go. It's already dark, but we don't want to leave it until midnight, when we'd be much more suspicious lurking around."

"We're not lurking." She folded her paper plate around her uneaten food. "You're checking on your sister."

They left Lori's car in the structure and took his rental to Summer's house. On the ride over, they kept things light and talked about their jobs and their families. They'd already revealed their single status to each other, but Lori wasn't offering any more details about her personal life.

He didn't want to dig too much further. She might wonder why he was asking. He had a life in New York, didn't he? He maneuvered off the freeway and squinted at the sign pointing toward Los Feliz Boulevard.

Lights from restaurants and businesses still open gave a glow to the street, lending a normalcy to this mission.

He turned off the boulevard, a sudden dread thrumming through his veins. As if sensing his anxiety, Lori tapped her fingers on his forearm.

She didn't even have to say a word. It had always been that way between them. He released a sigh and a little bit of tension with it when he turned onto Summer's block. He pulled up in front of the small house with the light still on in the front window.

Lori pointed to the empty driveway. "Does Summer have a car?"

"Yeah, but she could keep it in the garage. I've never been inside her place. I don't know her habits."

"But you know she lives alone."

"For sure." He cut the engine. "Maybe we'll get lucky and the front door will be unlocked. She was always careless about that kind of stuff."

They both exited the vehicle, and Cade stood on the sidewalk facing the house, hands on his hips. "We should probably do our breaking and entering around the back, away from neighbors' prying eyes."

"Let's try our luck first." Lori strode up to the house, rang the bell and tried the door. "I guess Summer isn't careless anymore."

They skirted the house along the side, and Cade lifted a latch on a wooden gate. The backyard boasted a small patio with a few dead potted plants and not much more. A slider led from the house to the patio, and he tried the door. "Locked."

Lori peeked around the other side of the house and crooked her finger at him. "Let's try that window."

She pointed at a small, frosted pane of glass, open a crack.

He said, "If we're going to break a window we might as well go big and break something I can fit through."

"Who said anything about breaking? I'm from East LA, *cabron*. I may have learned a few tricks from my brother and his friends." She grabbed his arm and pulled him toward the window. "Place your hands flat on the glass and push up. If there's any wiggle room, you can create some space at the bottom of the window frame and lift it out."

Grinning at her insult in Spanish, Cade reached over her and flattened his hands against the cool glass. He shoved the entire window up and lifted it from its track. "Got it."

"Try to maneuver it out."

With a little shifting and readjusting, he cleared the window from the track, grabbed the sides and lifted it free. As he leaned it against the side of the house, he said, "That was scarily easy." He straightened to his full height. "I hope you're not expecting me to go through that."

"Of course not. You're here for the muscle. Give me a boost."

Crouching down, he laced his fingers to create a cradle, and Lori placed one sneaker in his hands. He lifted her until her head cleared the window frame.

She said, "It's right over the tub. I'll be fine. A little higher."

He raised his hands, and she grabbed the ledge and hoisted herself through the opening. He got a good look at her backside as she wriggled through the space, and then her feet disappeared as if she'd been sucked into a time portal.

Too bad it didn't lead to a portal to the past, so he could correct all the mistakes he'd made with his first serious relationship…his first love.

"Hey!"

He started and focused on the oval of her face framed by the opening.

"I'll let you in at the front door."

He left the window propped up against the side of the house and jogged back to the front porch. Seconds later, he heard the click of the dead bolt and

Lori swung open the door, her dark eyes huge in her pale face.

His heart tumbled. "What's wrong?"

"I'm not sure. I glanced into a bedroom on my way to open the door and…" she twisted her fingers in front of her "…come have a look for yourself. Maybe it's nothing."

He shut the door behind him and followed her down a short hallway, his breath coming in short spurts. Lori had been to enough crime scenes to pick up on something amiss, and her alarm jolted him.

She turned into a room off the hallway, and he stumbled in behind her, his feet suddenly feeling like he was wearing clown shoes five sizes too big.

His gaze swept the room, lit from below by a lamp on its side near the bed. The messy bed drew his attention. Summer had never been a neat freak, but the disheveled covers looked as if they'd hosted a wrestling match.

He licked his lips and met Lori's glassy eyes for a split second. Then he charged out of the room calling his sister's name. He dipped his head into the kitchen, scanning the dirty dishes in the sink…and a broken glass on the floor.

With the adrenaline pumping through his body, he charged through the rest of the house. "Summer!"

He threw open a door that led to the attached garage, his fingers clawing for the light switch to verify the fact that her car was gone. He spun around and wandered back to the living room.

"Her car's gone. Maybe she left a mess and took off before she could pick up." Before she could pick up a broken glass on the kitchen floor?

Lori didn't reassure him. In fact, she said nothing at all as she crouched beside the front door, her back to him, her shoulders stiff.

Cade wiped the back of his hand across his mouth. "What's wrong?"

She twisted her head over her shoulder and whispered, "I found a bloody fingerprint."

Chapter Three

Cade listed to one side as if he couldn't keep steady on the pitching deck of a boat. Then he squared his shoulders and came toward her. He dropped to his knees in front of the door, and she circled the air in front of the latent print left in blood on the doorjamb—just like the print left at Courtney's house.

His blue eyes clouded. "That could be her print, right? Maybe she cut her finger on the glass she broke in the kitchen and touched the door frame on her way out."

Lori nodded but averted her eyes from his. She couldn't take the pleading in their depths. "Could be."

"Too bad we don't have your car. You can take the print now, couldn't you?"

She pushed to her feet, her hand on Cade's shoulder easing her way up. "I wouldn't do that, Cade. This scene needs to be processed. It's the same as the other situation I mentioned—there's some probable cause here. Summer's been gone for over twenty-four hours. Her phone is turned off. She missed a meeting with you. If you call the police now and tell them about the overturned lamp, the messed-up bed, the glass in the kitchen—and this bloody print—they'll come."

He stood up next to her and took her hand. "I want you to do it, Lori. I want you to be on the scene."

She squeezed his hand. "I think I can arrange that. Especially because…"

She trailed off, but Cade in his current state of mind didn't notice. She'd been about to remark on how much the scene at Summer's house resembled the house they'd processed earlier. Why no real evidence of a crime except for one fingerprint in blood? It's almost as if it was placed there on purpose.

She didn't actually know what the rest of the CSI team had discovered at Courtney's house. She didn't even know what she had yet with that print.

Cade called it in, using the words she put in his mouth for maximum response. A little over an hour later, she was working with the same team that had processed Courtney's house, except Detective Marino had replaced Detective Falco.

The detective made Cade wait in his rental car, and when Marino came back inside, he rolled his eyes at Lori.

She packed up the fingerprint kit one of the CSIs had brought to the scene for her, and sidled next to the detective. "What's up?"

"Mr. Cade Larson doesn't know much about his

sister, does he?" He waved one arm around the room. "The bed could be due to a restless sleep, same with the bedside lamp knocked over. She dropped a glass in the kitchen, cut her hand and left a bloody print on her way out."

"On her way out where? Urgent care? A hospital emergency room? Then why didn't she call her brother who's visiting from New York? Why didn't she cancel their dinner? Why is her phone turned off?"

Marino leveled a finger at her. "You were working too long on that task force for The Player. You could be a bona fide detective now."

"Are you making fun of me?" She raised an eyebrow and tilted her chin.

"Nope. There are definitely some issues with Summer's…disappearance, but young women go missing in this city daily. We're here at this scene because I know the brother is your friend and—" he jerked his thumb toward the front door "—that's Cade Larson from Larson Construction, isn't it?"

She gave Marino a stingy smile. Cade's name and connections always did and would have pull in LA. Cade's father was tight with the mayor, even though Mr. Larson no longer lived here. Cade probably could've thrown the Larson name around the station earlier and gotten the same result without breaking into his sister's house—but she was glad it had worked out this way.

"Yes, his and Summer's father is Lars Larson from Larson Construction."

"Then it doesn't much matter that the brother knows nothing about his sister's habits, and that she could be on a vacation off the grid. Money and power talk." Marino gave a shrug of his rounded shoulders.

A flash of heat claimed Lori's chest, as she rose to Cade's defense. "He doesn't know much about her habits because he lives across the country and he just got into the city. He arrived the day he and Summer were scheduled to have dinner."

Marino held out his palms. "Okay, okay. I'm just thinking he might be overreacting because he's feeling guilty."

Lori opened her mouth and then snapped it closed. She knew Cade felt guilty about not monitoring Summer more in his parents' absence, but Summer was an adult. They were all adults now, responsible for their own actions.

She could give Cade a lot more to feel guilty about, but she refused to go there with him. Hopefully, his sister would turn up unharmed, they could have a nice visit and Cade could return to his own corner of the country. She had exorcised him from her mind once. She could do it again.

She'd finished her part of the CSI but didn't want to mess up the chain of evidence by taking the prints back to the station in the car with the potential victim's brother. She located Sam, the photographer, and asked, "Can I ride back to the station with you? I don't have my car."

"Sure, give me ten."

Lori went outside and ducked beneath the yellow tape to put the fingerprint case in the van. When she turned, she almost bumped into Cade.

He nodded toward his sister's house. "Did they find anything else?"

"Not yet." She tapped the side of the van. "I'm going back to the station with the rest of the CSI team. Have to make sure the prints are protected."

"I'll follow you."

Did he think he could pump her for more information? If she had it, would she give it to him? If she had known someone on the inside of her brother's case, she would've done everything in her power to get a heads-up on the evidence. She expected no less from Cade.

"It's getting late, Cade." She touched his arm. "You don't have to follow. I'll tell you everything as soon as I learn it."

"Your car's still in the parking structure in Santa Monica. How are you going to collect it? I can drive you back."

"I can take an app car."

"By yourself?" His eyes widened. "To a parking structure in the middle of the night to then drive home alone to Venice? Not happening."

A little thrill ran up her spine. As self-sufficient as she'd always been, she'd adored that protective side of Cade. He'd protected her from everything right up until the end.

"I can't guarantee how long I'm going to be at the station, and I can't invite you up to the lab."

"I'll wait as long as it takes." He placed his hands on her shoulders. "I owe you. Without your suggestion tonight, I'd be cooling my heels in my hotel room waiting for forty-eight hours to have passed. Now, we're getting somewhere."

She blinked at the intensity of his eyes. "If you insist on waiting, at least get yourself some coffee so you have something to do in the car."

"Don't worry about me." He held up his cell phone. "I can always check emails from work. Just do what you have to do, and I'll be waiting for you in the parking lot of the station when you're done."

Nobody had waited around for her in quite a while. She could get used to this…but she'd better not. That phone in his hand with the emails waiting would take Cade back to New York soon enough.

He left the scene before the CSI van pulled out. She wanted to believe Detective Marino that Summer had taken off on her own. Lots of people wanted to disconnect and tune out these days. When her supervisor, Clive Stewart, had been identified as the notorious serial killer The Player, she'd wanted to take off and unplug for a while herself. Then there was Summer's drug use. She noticed Cade hadn't told the detective any of that. Maybe she had kicked the habit, but that didn't mean it hadn't gotten her in its clutches again.

By the time the van got to the Northeast Division, Cade's rental car was already sitting in the parking lot. Before she walked into the station, she made a detour to Cade's car and he buzzed down the window at her approach.

He stuck out a hand, clutching a coffee cup, and his head followed. "Not sure what you wanted, so I went with a straight coffee, black, and then you can add to it."

She took the cup from him, and their fingertips met. She had to grab the cup before it slipped through their hands. His touch had always caused her to quake, and nothing had changed. "Thank you. If the wait becomes too much, text me. I don't know how long I'll be. It could be minutes or it could be an hour."

He held up his coffee in one hand and a pastry bag in the other. "I'm good to go."

She left him in the parking lot and went upstairs to the lab with the prints she'd taken from Summer's house.

She hadn't gotten a response back from IAFIS on the other prints, not that she'd expected anything this soon. Only murder investigations got the rush treatment.

She got to work prepping the bloody print from Summer's place for submission to IAFIS. At a glance, that print did not look similar to the prints she'd gathered from the rest of the house—prints most likely belonging to Summer. The realization caused a flutter of fear in her chest.

The bloody print could belong to Summer's friend, someone at the house when she'd cut her hand on the glass in the kitchen. Someone there to help, not harm.

She worked for about twenty minutes, and by the time she finished, the other techs had left. She'd felt a little creeped out in the lab alone ever since she found out about Clive, but she was never really alone at the station. Even detectives worked a graveyard shift for the LAPD, and some spent that time at their desks going over evidence, doing research, reviewing mug shots.

When she packed up to leave, she poked her head into the room that housed Robbery-Homicide in an open layout. As expected, a few detectives populated the desks and a couple of patrol officers were hanging out.

She raised a hand. "I'm taking off."

They all glanced up and one of the officers asked her if she wanted him to walk her to her car.

She snorted. "I'm at a police station. Besides, I have a ride waiting for me, but thanks."

Was he still waiting for her? Cade had let her down only once, but it had been a devastating blow to her. She swallowed and felt light-headed when she saw his car parked in the same spot, a glow coming from the interior. He hadn't been kidding about getting some work done.

Lori tapped on the driver's-side window, and Cade glanced up. The locks popped and he jerked his thumb toward the passenger seat.

As she slid into the seat beside him, she inhaled the scent of warm banana bread. She flicked the paper bag on the center console. "You really know how to make yourself at home."

"I even got some work done." He held out the crumpled bag in his palm. "There's a little piece of banana bread left. Do you want it?"

"No, thanks, but that coffee sure helped." She snapped her seat belt and studied his profile in the muted light. "You didn't have to wait."

"You said that to me once before—I took you at your word and regretted it ever since." His lips twisted into a smile.

Was that how he remembered it? To cover her awkwardness, she grabbed the bag and fished out the bread. She stuffed the whole piece in her mouth.

Cade didn't even blink. He started the car and pulled out of the lot. "I suppose you didn't discover anything yet."

She swallowed and patted the sticky crumbs on her lips. "I just prepped the prints and submitted them to the national database. I also added them to our own local database of prints—faster read, but not as comprehensive. It's not a substitute for IAFIS by any means."

She jerked her head to the side when she heard Cade huff out a breath. "What?"

A half smile curved his mouth. "I like hearing you talk shop. I'm glad you found work that inspires you."

"Don't tell me you think it's cute." She crossed her arms in case he got any ideas.

"Not at all. Just makes me happy to know you found a calling." His hands clenched the steering wheel before he flexed his fingers. "It is your calling, right? Not just another way to help Danny?"

She tightened her jaw. What if it was? "I like the work. It has nothing to do with my brother."

"Okay, good. I'd hate to hear you'd let Danny control your life like…" He stopped and bit his lower lip.

Like she used to let Danny occupy all her thoughts and energy? She slumped in her seat and closed her eyes. "I'm tired."

He splayed his hands on the wheel. "Got it."

Cade drove the rest of the way without talking while she pretended to doze. How had she let him get under her skin so quickly?

When he pulled next to her car in the empty parking structure, she grabbed the door handle. "Thanks for the ride, Cade, and the dinner. I'll keep you informed if anything comes up."

She gave him a quick wave and slammed the door. She needed to put this relationship back on the right track—professional only. She couldn't afford to lose her heart to Cade Larson again.

And she couldn't afford to tell him about their child.

THE FOLLOWING MORNING, Lori showered and dressed for work. She hadn't gotten rid of Cade as easily as she'd thought when she'd hightailed it out of his car and into her own in the parking garage last night. He'd followed her home to her house on the Venice Canals and waited until she'd crossed the wooden bridge, his headlights illuminating her way. When she reached her street, he flashed his lights.

Instead of giving her the warm fuzzies, his gesture had sent a wave of panic crashing through her body. The man could snap his fingers and she'd morph into a gooey puddle at his expensively shod size elevens.

She gave herself a grimace as she scraped her hair into a severe ponytail. There would be no melting if she could avoid him.

Once they found Summer crashing at a friend's place with an injured hand, Cade could return to New York, and she could return to…what? Work, worry over Danny, her mother's phone calls gushing about her grandchildren in Texas and The Hague— not about the secret grandchild Lori put up for adoption after she'd graduated from high school. The child she'd never mentioned to Cade.

It could be worse.

By the time she arrived at the Northeast Division, she'd shaken off her poor, pitiful me mood and she breezed into the lab. She hung up her jacket and purse and sidled next to Josh, working at the table in the middle of the room. "You missed some action last night—two potential crime scenes. Skiing in Big Bear?"

"I heard, and yeah, my kids wanted to catch the last of the snow up there before the pack melts." He rubbed his eyes. "But the drive home last night? Brutal. Two missing women?"

"Maybe." Lori crossed the room to her desk and booted up her computer. "Some similarities to the scenes. I processed and prepped the prints and sent them to IAFIS."

"Did you submit them to the local, too?"

"I did and—" she scooted in closer to her laptop, her breath catching in her throat "—hello. Looks like I got a hit on the local database already."

Josh grunted. "Your lucky day."

Lori brought up the report, and her eyes widened. "This can't be right."

"Don't tell me. We got The Player's prints again."

Her gaze darted between the bloody print from Courtney's house and the prints from Summer's. Her heart hammered in her chest as she stared at the irrefutable evidence.

Summer Larson had left a fingerprint in blood at Courtney Jessup's place.

Chapter Four

Cade stepped out of the shower and tucked the white hotel towel around his waist. As he brushed his teeth in front of the mirror, his phone rang on the vanity and he dropped his toothbrush in the sink as he lunged for it. His disappointment lasted less than a second when he saw Lori's name on the display instead of Summer's.

"Did they find her?" His voice echoed off the tiles of the cavernous bathroom, amplifying the sound of his fear.

"No, but..." Lori took a deep breath, which made Cade's heart rate ratchet up a few more notches. "Look, I discovered something weird this morning when I came into the station. I want to talk to you about it—in person. Lunch?"

"Yeah, yeah, lunch—" Cade slicked back his wet hair from his forehead with one unsteady hand "—but you can't leave me hanging, Lori. What did you discover?"

"Does the name Courtney Jessup mean anything to you?"

"No." The mirror had steamed up again, and he rubbed a hole in the center of it with his fist, as if that could clear the confusion in his mind. "Does she have something to do with Summer?"

Lori coughed. "Remember I told you about the other missing woman and how her friend had broken into her place?"

"That's what gave you the idea that I should do the same at Summer's place. What about her?"

"That woman was Courtney Jessup, and I lifted a bloody fingerprint from her house just like I did at Summer's."

"Yeah?" The towel slipped from Cade's waist and dropped to the floor, pooling around his feet, but he stood frozen, hanging on every one of Lori's words.

Lori blew out a breath. "The bloody print at Courtney's place matches Summer's print. Summer was at Courtney's place."

Cade shook his head back and forth, flicking droplets of water onto the vanity. "That's not possible. Why would Summer be at the crime scene of another house? Are you implying she had something to do with Courtney's disappearance?"

"Not at all. I don't know what it means, Cade. I double-checked a few times to make sure I hadn't somehow entered the wrong print for Summer, but there it is. Summer's fingerprint was definitely at Courtney's house."

"Maybe they were abducted together." Cade grabbed the damp towel and clutched it to his chest. "Maybe Summer was injured and taken at Courtney's, and then their kidnapper returned to Summer's house to…I don't know, steal something or make her get her car and purse."

"That could be." She paused. "I turned the information over to the detective on the case, but I wanted you to know. You have a right to know, but I have to get back to work right now. Let's have lunch… near Los Feliz. Bring Summer's key. I saw you take it last night."

His grip on his phone loosened for the first time since he picked it up. He knew what Lori had in mind, and he was game. "Give me a time and place, and I'll be there…with the key."

CADE SPENT THE morning on the phone with his assistant and working on a report for a new development, which he'd have to check for errors later. Lori's bombshell news occupied his mind, as he turned it over and over in his head.

Summer obviously knew Courtney. Perhaps the two women had been surprised together. The intruder had a weapon, but the women fought back. Maybe Summer left a bloody print at the scene as a clue. The kidnapper could've then forced Summer, or both women, back to Summer's house and another struggle ensued there.

That had to be the explanation.

He checked the time on his laptop and shut it down. He slid the computer into his bag in case he and Lori needed it for…sleuthing? He knew Lori intended to look into this on her own.

She may work for the police department, but it didn't mean she trusted the police. Her brother's run-ins with the cops had left a bad taste in her mouth, even though everyone else could see that Danny instigated the issues. You couldn't say that to Lori though. *He* couldn't say it to her. He'd tried a few times, and his efforts had ended in arguments between them.

Now Lori's distrust of the police would benefit him. He knew he could count on her to share every aspect of this investigation with him, and he planned to take advantage of that.

He should've gotten a hotel closer to Summer's house to save him the trek across LA, but he preferred staying near the coast and he had thought he'd have a couple of dinners with Summer, check on his parents' home in Malibu and head back to New York. He couldn't have been more wrong.

It took him over an hour to get to the restaurant on Los Feliz Boulevard and another fifteen minutes to find parking, but his efforts paid off. When he walked into the bustling café, Lori popped up from a table by the window and waved her hand at him. As the hostess approached him, he pointed to Lori and said, "I'm joining her."

He'd searched for Lori on social media in the past,

but she didn't have much of a presence online. He didn't know what he would've done if he'd contacted her, anyway, but seeing her now made him regret not trying harder.

Over the years, he'd tried to dismiss his feelings for Lori as a shallow high school crush, but he'd never really convinced himself of that. How could something surface level seep into your pores and stay with you for almost ten years?

He threaded his way through the other tables to reach her and pulled out the chair across from her. Jerking his thumb at the window, he said, "Good spot."

"I got here a little early." With her fingernail, she pinged her glass of soda, which had to be Diet Coke. She'd been addicted to the drink. "I would've ordered you an iced tea, but I didn't want to presume. You used to drink the stuff by the gallon, the only teenage boy I knew who didn't guzzle sugary soft drinks."

"You know my father wouldn't allow that stuff in our house." He rolled his eyes and shook his finger. "No refined sugar, son."

She toyed with her straw. "I wasn't sure if you still followed your father's rules."

A flash of heat claimed his chest. "You know, old habits die hard—not that any of that health stuff our dad mandated ever had an impact on Summer."

The waitress approached, and he ordered his iced tea while they both told her they needed more time with the menu.

When the waitress spun away to her next table, Lori hunched forward. "I checked the print again, and it's a match. Summer was definitely at Courtney's place."

"What did the detective say?"

She lifted and dropped her shoulders quickly. "He's not going to tell me, is he? They'll probably investigate the contacts of the two women to find out how they might have been connected."

"Are we going to, what?" He spread his hands. "Conduct our own parallel investigation?"

"It's either that or you can wait for the police to share information with you about the case when they're good and ready." Her lips clamped around her straw and she took a sip of her drink. "Is that what you want? The police never told us about that unidentified print at Elena's house. They never told Danny or his lawyer—not until they got the confession out of Danny. Do you want to go down that road?"

"I don't want to be kept in the dark, but I don't want to get you in trouble."

Placing a hand against her chest, Lori widened her eyes and fluttered her lashes. *"Moi?"*

The waitress returned, saving him from cataloguing all the ways this could go wrong for Lori, but all she'd done so far was give him a heads-up on the print. He had a right to know that information.

After they ordered their sandwiches, Lori folded her hands on the table. "Did you bring the key to Summer's house?"

He patted the chest pocket of the flannel he'd thrown on over his T-shirt this morning when he left the hotel. "Got it right here. What's the plan? Can we get into Summer's place after the search last night, or is that off-limits?"

"Wasn't much of a crime scene to process. They're done with it, but it doesn't mean we are." She tapped a finger on the table. "Now that we know Summer knew Courtney, we have a better idea of what to look for in her house."

"What about the police? Will they be doing the same?"

"They can go a step beyond us. They can get Courtney's and Summer's phone records. There's no evidence of a murder, so they won't put a rush on those records. They can also question Courtney's friend. Of course, we can do that, too." She held up a hand as he opened his mouth. "There's no law against talking to Trey Ferrar on our own. He might open up to you more when he finds out your sister's print was at his friend's place."

"I don't know if that's a great idea. This guy, Trey, might think Summer had something to do with the disappearance of Courtney—and we know that's not true." Cade abraded his knuckles across his jaw. "I know how I'd feel if it were the other way around—if Courtney's bloody print had been found at Summer's house. That didn't happen, did it?"

Lori paused as the waitress dropped off their baskets of food. She picked up a French fry and waved it in the air. "I submitted the print from Summer's house to the national database but haven't received any match back yet and it didn't match up to anything we have locally—including Courtney's print."

Cade let out the breath he'd been holding and took a bite of his sandwich. He didn't know what Lori expected to find from searching Summer's house that the cops wouldn't uncover from her phone records, but he couldn't stand around waiting for the police to fill him in on his missing sister. Action beat inaction anytime.

Cade slurped up the tea at the bottom of his glass. "If we're going to turn Summer's house upside down, we'd better get going. You have to get back to work at some point."

"I have some time. I worked over the weekend, so I bought myself some hours off during the week."

Pushing his food away, Cade asked, "What exactly are we looking for that the police wouldn't notice?"

"The police did a forensics sweep, but we don't even know if a crime has been committed. That's a different type of search. They may get Summer's phone records, but there's no urgency...yet."

"Even after finding her prints at the other missing woman's place?"

"A lot of people go missing in LA, Cade, some even know each other. That's why you have to take matters into your own hands sometimes." Lori's lips formed a thin line, and her jaw tightened.

Did she really still believe if she'd been able to investigate the murder of Danny's girlfriend that she could've exonerated him?

He held up his hands. "You don't have to convince me. I felt frustrated at the station yesterday when I couldn't do anything to help Summer. You changed all that."

A pink tinge touched her cheeks, and she grabbed the check. "You got dinner last night, so lunch is on me."

He gave up easily. Uncomfortable with his family's wealth, Lori had always been conscious of paying her own way, and she hadn't seemed to have changed.

Lori followed him to Summer's house, and his gaze flicked across the front as he pulled up to the curb. When Lori joined him on the sidewalk, he asked, "No crime scene tape?"

"The police are done with the search. We're not going to disturb anything." She tugged on the sleeve of his shirt. "Let's go."

Cade fished Summer's house key out of the pocket of his shirt, as he strode toward the porch. He unlocked the bottom lock. The cops hadn't had a key to lock the dead bolt when they left, so they'd left it unlocked. Pushing open the door, he held his breath. Maybe she'd just step into the room, tossing her long blond hair over her shoulder, blue eyes twinkling with mischief.

The silence that met him splashed his face with cold water.

He blinked. "She's not here."

Lori touched his shoulder. "We'll find her. You look out here and I'll check her bedroom."

"What are we looking for?" He ran a hand through his hair, his eyes darting around the room.

"Anything a little unusual." Lori held up her hand and ticked off her fingers. "Diary, for sure. Receipts, business cards, address book, even scraps of papers with names or numbers."

He shoved his hands in his pockets, his feet rooted to the floor. Did he want to know any of Summer's private business? "If she had a diary, the police would've taken it."

"They don't even know if a crime has been committed." Lori shrugged. "Maybe we'll get lucky, but we're not going to find anything if we don't get started."

Cade felt a flush suffuse his face. She must've noticed his reluctance. His family had always looked the other way when it came to Summer's secrets, his parents covering them up to avoid embarrassment. Maybe that was why his sister had wound up missing in LA with no family members in town.

He willed his feet to move, one plodding step following the next. "I'll start with the kitchen."

Lori nodded once and headed down the hallway to Summer's bedroom.

Cade yanked open the first cabinet on his right and studied the mismatched plates and bowls, stacked into little, leaning towers. One corner of his mouth twitched. His mother would get an anxiety attack just looking at this hodgepodge…probably why Summer did it.

His other sister, Sarah, had always conformed to what Mom wanted, or maybe Sarah wanted it, too— that well-ordered existence of matching dishes and matching shoes and fake smiles that pretended that was all anyone ever needed in life to be happy.

Had he fallen into that trap, too? It hadn't been that way in high school when he'd dated Lori. She'd encouraged an aspect of his personality that he'd previously shut down, made him feel alive. Had he been living in some kind of alternate reality since then? None of the women he'd dated in New York had ever made him feel the way he'd felt about Lori.

He blinked. Staring at dishes wouldn't help Summer now. He slammed the cupboard doors and pulled open a drawer. Sifting through the jumbled mess of paper clips, pens, magnets and sticky notes, he thought that this had to be more of what Lori meant.

As he squinted at a pink square of paper stuck to his fingertip, Lori called from the bedroom, "I found something."

His heart jumped and he spun away from the open drawer, the pink sticky note still attached to his finger as he rushed to the bedroom. His gaze tracked over the rumpled bed covers and the gaping drawers and landed on Lori standing on a chair facing the closet. She'd made a lot more progress than he had.

She peered over her shoulder at him, cupping

something in the palm of her hand. "I think this might be important."

He entered the room, stepping over a pillow on the floor. "What is it?"

Turning, she hopped down from the chair and stretched out her open hand. "A key."

"A key?" He tilted his head to one side and plucked the small silver key from her hand. "Why do you think this is important? It could be a key to anything, although…"

Lori cut him off. "It's important because she hid it. I could see tossing a key in a drawer, but she secreted this away in a shoebox. It was taped to the inside of the box."

"Okay." Cade chewed his bottom lip as he ran a thumb along the teeth of the key.

"Th-there's something else, Cade."

He glanced at her face, her soft lips pulled down into a frown, and his pulse quickened. Then he dropped his gaze to the shoe dangling from her other hand. "You found a shoe in a shoebox?"

"I wish that's all it was." She shoved her fingers into the toe of the shoe and pulled out a plastic bag, which crackled between her fingers. "I also found this."

He peered at the small baggie pinched between her thumb and forefinger, zeroing in on the powdery white substance inside. His jaw felt tight as he eked the word out between his lips. "Drugs."

Chapter Five

Lori curled her hand around the baggie and squeezed her fist. She hadn't wanted to tell Cade that his sister was using again, but he shouldn't run from the truth. The Larson family always ran from the truth.

His family's insistence on covering up every unpleasant blip in the road had driven a wedge between her and Cade, and it was one of the many reasons she'd never told him about her pregnancy. His parents would've gone ballistic.

He sank to the foot of the rumpled bed and braced his elbows on his knees, his head hanging down. "She told me she was clean."

"They always say that." She sat beside him and rubbed a circle on his back. The gesture took her back to their teen years when they'd console each other about their errant siblings. Now Danny was in prison for manslaughter and Summer was missing under suspicious circumstances.

Once you added drugs to the mix of a person who'd disappeared, it put a whole new twist on the situation. She flattened the baggie on her knee. "What do you think it is? What was she using?"

"According to what she told me, nothing, but this could be anything, right? Cocaine, heroin, GHB, fentanyl, Molly."

She raised her eyebrows. "You know your street drugs."

"And how do you think I got so knowledgeable?" He clasped his hands in front of him. "Trial by fire trying to help Summer conquer her addictions."

The baggie expanded as she spread open her fingers, the white powder shifting in the creases of the plastic. "Why do you think she hid the drugs with the key? They must be connected."

"Really?" He jerked his head to the side. "Maybe she used that box to hide everything. Did you find anything else inside?"

"Just the shoes." She kicked at the suede pump on the floor, tipping it over. "If I recall correctly, that's hardly her style."

Cade hunched his shoulders. "I wouldn't really know, but I do think I know something about this key."

"Really?"

Holding it up, he said, "It looks like a safe deposit box key, doesn't it?"

"You're asking me?" She drilled a finger into her chest. "I've never had a safe deposit box in my life and wouldn't know the first thing about what a key

to one should look like, although I imagine it would
be on the small side…like this one."

"Exactly." He bobbled the key in the palm of his
hand and it winked as it caught the light from the
window. "Why would a safe deposit box be linked to
drugs? She wouldn't be putting drugs in the bank. In
fact, I find it hard to believe she put her stash in the
toe of a shoe, in a shoebox, on a shelf in her closet.
You're standing on a chair to reach it, and Summer's
not much taller than you are. It's not a convenient
location."

"Unless that's her backup. Maybe the person who
abducted her took her drugs, too, drugs she kept
closer at hand."

"That doesn't make me feel any better." Cade
pushed off the bed and took a turn around the room.
"And it still doesn't answer the question as to why
she hid a key to a safe deposit box and a baggie of
drugs in the same place."

"You're sure it's a safe deposit box and not some
locker somewhere?" Lori dipped to the floor and
swept up the shoe. Running her fingers across the
suede, she said, "It just looks like a small key to me.
It could be anything."

Cade framed the key with two fingers and held
it up. "Trust me. I know safe deposit boxes, and I'm
sure my parents set her up with one."

"Do you know where Summer banks?"

"I don't have a clue, but she must have some bank
receipts around here. Even if she does everything

online, she's gotta have some ATM receipts tucked away somewhere. It's not as if she has a great filing system." Cade tucked the key into the front pocket of his jeans. "And I know just the place to look."

Lori waved the bag of drugs in the air. "What do we do with this?"

"We're not turning it over to the police." Cade stopped at the bedroom door and gripped either side of the doorjamb.

Lori scooted off the bed, dropping the shoe to the floor, where it thunked loudly. She thought he might say something like this. "The more information the police have, the faster they can find Summer."

"You, of all people, are telling me this?" He cranked his head over his shoulder. "Once they know she's involved with drugs, they'll lose the urgency to investigate her disappearance—not that they have much of an urgency now. You know how it is, Lori. They'll figure she's off doing drugs somewhere or ran away with her druggie friends. Let's look into this ourselves first."

She did know how he felt. Even though she worked with the police every day and respected the hell out of them, her family had been burned before by detectives who wanted the easy answer and took it.

She let out a slow breath. "Sure, we'll do it your way for now."

His shoulders slumped. "Good. Do you want to

clean up in here while I claw through Summer's junk drawer in the kitchen?"

"Go for it."

When he exited the room, Lori straightened the bed and stuffed some items hanging over the drawers back inside. She perched on the edge of the bed and swept a sleep mask, a packet of condoms and a bottle of melatonin into an open drawer on Summer's nightstand. Why did Summer need melatonin to sleep on top of everything else she might be taking?

As she began to slide the drawer closed, a blue-and-green card stuck in the back corner caught her eye. She plucked it free and held it up to the light from the open blinds at the window. She read aloud from the card. "'Brighter Days Recovery Center, Reed Dufrain, Center Coordinator.'"

Pinching the card between her fingers, Lori bounced up from the bed and called out, "Cade?"

He yelled back, "I found it. I found her bank."

She joined him in the kitchen, where a drawer gaped open, revealing a jumbled mess of odds and ends.

He waved some papers in the air. "First Western Bank. Figures, since that's where my parents bank, and I still bank there due to habit. My parents probably set up the account and safe deposit box for her."

"I found something, too." She flicked the card. "Did Summer ever talk about rehab? She had this card in the drawer of her bedside table for Brighter

Days Recovery Center. There's a rehab facility in To-panga Canyon and a treatment center in Hollywood."

Cade leaned in, his breath warm on her cheek. "She's been in and out of rehab, but I've never heard of this place—not that she told me much about her recovery process. I guess it didn't work out for her, or she wouldn't have had those drugs in her closet."

"That's weird, to have a card for a treatment center and a stash of drugs in your place."

"Is it?" Cade slid the drawer closed with a sharp snap. "It's not uncommon for addicts to fall off the wagon and even go back and forth. Didn't that happen to Danny?"

Tears pricked the backs of her eyes, and she ran a hand under her nose. "Danny never tried to stop using, and he certainly didn't have the money for an expensive recovery spa like this one in Topanga. His treatment center was prison."

Cade squeezed her shoulder. "I'm sorry. I didn't mean it like that."

Her sniff turned into a smile. "I know you didn't. It still might be worth checking out this Brighter Days Recovery Center and talking to—" she squinted at the card "—Reed Dufrain."

"First things first. Let's see what Summer has in her safe deposit box that she'd keep the key hidden away with her drugs. I hope she doesn't have more drugs in there. That could be a legal problem."

"How do you plan to get into her safe deposit box? I know I said I didn't have one, but that doesn't mean

I don't have some inkling of how they work. Don't you have to be an authorized user or something? Doesn't the bank have signatures on file and yours has to match?"

"You should know by now how the Larson family does things. First Western is my bank—it's my parents' bank and I'm one hundred percent sure they opened that account for my sister and they're coapplicants with her. I can also guarantee my father knows someone on the board and has done a favor for him or her in the past."

He must've noticed the sour look on her face because he spread his hands and said, "That's the way of the world. In this case, it's to our benefit."

"I know." She leveled a finger at him. "Don't think I forgot all the special treatment I got hanging out with you and the other kids at Brentwood Prep."

"At times like these—" he shoved the bank receipts in his pocket "—those connections come in handy. Speaking of connections, do you have the entire day off?"

"That doesn't have to do with connections, rich boy." She slugged his biceps, meeting rock-solid muscle. "That comes from putting in the extra work."

He glanced at his phone. "We still need to get over to the bank before it closes. Even I can't force the bank to open for my personal needs."

"I bet your dad could."

"And you'd be right."

"Are you going to tell your parents about Summer? What if they've been trying to contact her?"

"Not yet. My father would make this all about him, and they rarely call Summer. They've always taken a hands-off approach to her and her issues, or have just thrown money at them. I'll reach out to them at the appropriate time—this isn't it."

He dangled his key between them. "Ready? We can't keep following each other all over LA. Leave your car here, and I'll drive to the bank."

"Is her branch nearby?"

"I looked it up. Close enough."

They locked up Summer's house, and then Lori slid into the passenger seat of Cade's rental. Sitting next to Cade in a car like this caused the memories to come at her fast and hard. They'd spent a lot of time in Cade's car in high school. They couldn't meet at her small house in Pacoima, jam-packed with people, and she'd been uneasy around the opulence of his house, on the coast in Malibu.

She cleared her throat. "I'm still not sure how you hope to get into Summer's safe deposit box."

"We'll figure it out when we get there." He tapped his finger on her thigh. "Don't you trust me?"

Years ago, that would've been a loaded question. Today? She'd made it through her naive teenage years, and Cade had developed into a man under his own agency. Hadn't he?

"I trust the power of the Larson name. How's

that?" She slid a glance to the side just in time to see his jaw harden.

Gripping the steering wheel with both hands, he said, "It has to be good enough…for now."

And the Larson name hadn't failed them, although she had to give some credit to Cade's take-charge manner that combined smooth coercion with a friendly insistence. It had taken a few phone calls and Cade's assurance that he had Summer's key, with her permission, but they'd made it to the bank's safe deposit vault alone with Summer's box in front of them.

As soon as the door closed with a whisper, on the woman who'd ushered them into the inner sanctum, Cade flipped open the lid of the long box.

Lori hovered beside him to peer into the metal container. Rolled-up papers that looked like old stock certificates nestled in the box, along with some pieces of jewelry that sparkled like fire in the low lights of the room.

She snatched one of the certificates from the box and smoothed it out on the table. "These must be old. Companies don't even issue certificates anymore."

Cade drilled his finger in the center of the paper before she let go and it rolled up again against his hand. "Pretty sure these are from our grandparents. I have a few of them myself."

"The jewelry?" Lori hooked a finger around a diamond necklace and lifted it from the box. "I'm assuming this is real or it wouldn't be here."

"It's real. Again, these are pieces from my grandmother's collection that she left to Summer and Sarah." Cade hunched over the box and sifted through the contents.

As the papers ran through his fingers, Lori spotted a familiar blue-and-green pattern. "Wait. What's that?"

"What?" Cade rested his hands on either side of the box, and Lori dipped her hand inside to retrieve the card.

Running her thumb across the embossed lettering on the front of the card, she said, "This is the same card for the Brighter Days Recovery Center I found in her nightstand drawer. Why would she put a business card for a rehab center in a safe deposit box?"

"I don't know why my sister does half the stuff she does. Maybe it wound up in here by accident."

"Because you keep a business card with heirloom jewelry and old stock certificates?" Lori bit her lip and flipped the card over.

Cade fanned through the papers in the box. "And a bunch of other papers. She could've swept it up with this stuff."

"Who are Diana, Chelsea and Karenna?" She held out the card to Cade. "All those names are on the back of this card. Is this Summer's handwriting?"

He scooted closer to her, his shoulder pressing against hers, his presence making her slightly dizzy in the small confines of the room.

"That is Summer's handwriting, and I've never

heard her mention those names. That's not surprising though—I couldn't even give the police any names to contact." He ran a finger along the edge of the card. "Do you think it's important?"

"I think it's important that she felt it necessary to lock up this card with these names in a safe deposit box with priceless diamonds."

He flicked the necklace in the box. "I wouldn't say these are priceless."

"You know what I mean." Lori nudged his arm with her elbow, just to get him out of her space. Did he realize the havoc he was causing in her brain… and her body? "I think we should hang on to this card. It's the only thing in this box that doesn't make sense."

"I agree." He rubbed the back of his hand along his forehead. "I'm just happy there are no drugs in here."

"If we could get her phone records, maybe we could match up some of these first names with people in her contacts. Then we could reach out to them to find out what's going on with her." She shoved the card in her purse. "You don't have any of those golden Larson contacts with her cell provider, do you?"

"Not that I know of." He carefully rolled up the stock certificates. "Is that something the police could do?"

"They can, but like I said before, there's no evidence of a homicide. They're in no hurry on this one." She scooped up the necklace and dangled it from her fingers, watching the rainbow sparks dance across the bank of safe deposit drawers. "Are you re-thinking giving them info on the drugs?"

"That's not going to give them a greater sense of urgency. In fact, the drugs are going to give them an excuse to back off. Both of us have seen this play out before." He held out his hand for the necklace. "Drug use equals throwaway person."

She dropped the heavy piece in his palm. "I hear ya. It's definitely one of the reasons why they jumped on Danny so fast."

Cade slid the box home and buzzed in the banker. Together, they secured the box and left the bank. He turned to her in the car. "Dinner later?"

Her pulse fluttered despite her best efforts to re-main calm and cool. She thought her visceral re-sponse to Cade at their first meeting had been due to the time that had passed. Anyone would be excited to see a high school flame, his or her first love, the father of her only child. That was why high school reunions spelled trouble for so many people.

But the spark she'd felt when she saw him in the lobby of the station had been growing into a full-on fire and if she didn't watch herself, she'd be in the middle of an inferno. But if she ran now, he'd see right through her.

She lifted one shoulder and dropped it quickly. "Sure, I can do dinner."

Her cheeks burned at the half smile that quirked

the side of his mouth. He'd seen right through her anyway.

"Let's get your car at Summer's and we'll discuss the where and when via text later. I'm going to try to do some work."

As Cade pulled out of the bank's parking lot, Lori fished the card for Brighter Days out of her purse. "I'm going to look this up online. Maybe Summer is there for rehab, and she's not supposed to answer her phone or have contact with anyone."

"And Courtney? Why were Summer's prints at her house?"

Lori tapped the edge of the card on the dashboard. "Maybe Courtney's in the same place. They know each other and decided to get treatment together."

"We don't know if they knew each other. The detectives haven't told you that yet, right?" He slid a glance her way, as if he suspected she was holding out on him.

She'd lied to Cade only once, even though it had been a whopper.

"They haven't told me anything." She traced a line over her lips. "They keep a lot to themselves."

"What about going to the source? You told me Courtney had a friend who reported her disappearance."

"Yeah, Trey. I can track him down. We can keep it on the sly. The department wouldn't appreciate my sleuthing on my own, but they can't control everything I do on my off hours."

"Like searching Summer's place and checking out her safe deposit box? I'll never tell." Cade put his finger to his lips.

She bounced her knuckle against the window. "Just drop me off and text me about dinner. I'm going to run back to the station for an hour."

He cruised to a stop across the street from her car, then parked in front of Summer's house and left the engine running as she opened the door.

She waved her hand at him. "See you later."

She jogged across the street, feeling his eyes following her. As she approached her car, she tripped to a stop, her hand covering her mouth.

Someone had slashed all four of her tires.

Chapter Six

Cade noticed the flat tires on Lori's car before she stumbled to a halt. One flat tire he could understand, but two, possibly four? He scrambled from his car.

He reached Lori just when she dropped to a crouch near her front driver's-side wheel. She turned her head over her shoulder. "Someone slashed them, Cade, all of them."

Running a finger along the smooth gap, he swore. "That they did. Do you have any enemies? Someone who would follow you here?"

"Enemies? No, of course not." She rose to her feet and squinted at the end of the street, her nostrils flaring. "It's because I'm here, at Summer's house. Don't you get it? Nobody followed me. Someone was watching Summer's house for some reason, and wants to warn me off, warn *us* off."

Cade felt a little buzz of apprehension at the back of his neck, and slapped it with his palm. "Who would care if we were here? The police were already here."

"The same person who knows where she is. There's nothing they can do about the cops showing up. But us?" Lori folded her arms and hunched her shoulders.

He couldn't go down this risky path with her. This might be her life, working alongside serial killers, visiting her brother in prison—but it wasn't his. "Hadn't you just convinced yourself that Summer and Courtney were in rehab?"

"That was before someone sliced my tires—two of which were brand-new."

"You need to call the cops. Does the LAPD come out for flat tires these days?"

"Not normally, but I'm one of them—sort of. They'll respond and take a report. I'll need it for the insurance anyway." She flicked her fingers in his direction. "You can head back to your hotel. I'll meet you later."

His eyebrows shot up. "Are you nuts? I'm not leaving you on this street with four slashed tires. You're going to need a tow, and then you'll be without a car. It's too late in the day for a garage to replace all your tires and get your car back to you. Call the cops, and then call your roadside service, if you have it."

"I do." She slipped her phone from her purse.

"I'll wait with you until the cops take a report and the tow truck driver hauls away your car. Then I'll drive you home. *Then* we'll have dinner."

She looked up from her phone. "What about work?"

"I think this is more important." He cocked his

head at her. Did she really think he'd leave her stranded here so he could get a few hours of work in before dinner? He must've been a worse boyfriend than he'd remembered.

Lori rolled her shoulders and tapped her phone display. "Cade to the rescue."

"Is that a problem?"

She held up her finger and started talking into her cell.

Forty minutes later, a cop car and a tow truck bookended Lori's car. As the fresh-faced cop snapped her notebook shut, she said, "There's not much we can do about it, Lori, but you can have the report for insurance purposes."

"Thanks, Jen. I hope it's covered as vandalism, or something."

Jen started to follow her partner back to their patrol car and spun around. "Be careful. Takes a lot of effort to gouge four tires like that. Someone must really have a grudge against you. This is no teenage prank."

Cade shifted his stance toward Lori and placed a hand on her back. This was all she needed to fire up her imagination and paranoia…and his.

"Does your brother have ties on the outside?" Jen bit her bottom lip, maybe afraid she'd said too much.

Lori's back stiffened beneath his hand. "My brother's connections didn't have anything to do with this."

"He's a member of the Norteños, isn't he?" Jen stood her ground, her eyes meeting Lori's.

Lori's back positively vibrated, and her voice grated. "Why would you think that? He and his friends ran wild, but they weren't in a gang."

"Norteños is a prison gang, not a street gang." Jen threw her hands out to her sides and said, "Hey, everyone has to survive inside, and if they don't play by the rules…sometimes people suffer on the outside."

"If it is something like that, it's because Danny wouldn't join the gang."

"If he didn't join, he'd be dead."

"Thanks for taking the report, Jen."

Jen shrugged and ducked into the patrol car, where her partner waited. Lori watched Jen and her partner drive off through narrowed eyes.

Jen must not know Lori very well. She didn't allow anyone to question her brother.

The beeping sound as the tow truck operator lifted Lori's car onto the back of the truck cut through the silence between them.

Cade rubbed a circle on Lori's back. "Could Jen be right? Maybe your brother didn't play ball with someone, so this gang, Norteños, took it out on you."

She lurched away from him. "I'm gonna talk to the driver."

Cade slid into the driver's seat of his rental and watched Lori out the window. Danny had always had her back when they were kids, when her dad worked long hours in construction and her mom worked as a nurse's aide on the graveyard shift at the hospital. Danny had encouraged Lori's studies and had seen her safely home from the library. When the tables had turned and Danny needed Lori's help, she hadn't hesitated.

Cade always believed Danny manipulated Lori at the end, and he knew manipulation firsthand. His sister was a master. Maybe Summer was manipulating him right now.

As Lori approached his car, he curled his hands around the steering wheel. He didn't have to worry about her picking up the discussion about Danny.

As she snapped her seat belt, she said, "He's taking it to a tire shop near the station. I'm going to pick it up after work tomorrow."

"Don't worry about it. I'll give you a ride to work in the morning."

"You don't have to go through all this trouble, you know." She pinned her hands between her knees, as they bounced up and down.

"Why wouldn't I?" He covered her hands with one of his. "You've gone above and beyond to help me find Summer. It's the least I can do. Let's not keep track of who's doing what for whom."

"Deal. So, why do you think my tires were slashed?" She dropped her gaze to her hands. "Do you really think it might have something to do with Danny?"

"Never occurred to me until Officer Jen mentioned it." He pulled away from the curb, giving

Summer's house one last glance. "Do you know much about Danny's life in prison?"

"I visit him, but I'm sure he's not giving me an accurate picture of what happens behind bars. Why would he?"

"And the gang?"

Lori sighed and leaned her head against the window. "Jen's right. There are two Latino gangs that predominate in the California prison system—the Norteños and the Sudeños, and everyone knows you have a better chance of survival when you affiliate with a prison gang. They're the ones who offer protection, get you privileges, have connections with the guards. But there's always a price to pay."

"And if you don't pay it?"

She scooped her hair back from her face. "Not sure. Are you asking me if the price might be harassment of family members on the outside? Maybe. Seems strange that they nailed my car in front of Summer's house, though, doesn't it? Because of the location, it seems much more likely that this has some connection to your sister and not my brother."

"I'm not saying it doesn't." He splayed his hands on the wheel. "It's not like we found anything in her safe deposit box, or even in the house. She had a small amount of drugs, not exactly a huge stash that someone would want to collect."

"We have the card from Brighter Days. It must mean something to her if she stuck it in the bank."

She folded her arms over her purse in her lap, as if protecting the cards there.

"Unless, like I said, she swept it up with other papers and put it there inadvertently. Summer doesn't exactly have a stellar system of filing...or anything else."

"We need to talk to Trey." She swiveled in her seat to face him. "Ask him about Brighter Days."

"I'm sure the police already asked him about Summer, right? I mean, her print was found at Courtney's place." He flicked on the windshield wipers to sweep away a few scattered raindrops that had shimmered in the lights on the freeway.

"Yeah, but what if Trey was protecting Courtney, like you're trying to protect Summer? Maybe Trey didn't tell the cops everything he knew about his friend, and maybe he doesn't know that Summer has a connection to Brighter Days. He'd tell us though."

"Do you know how to contact him?"

She snorted. "I can get his contact info from work. I'm the one who took his prints."

"Maybe I should talk to him—keep you out of it. My sister is missing. His friend is missing. We have a bond, and maybe he'll open up to me."

"I'd like to be there. He already knows me. I already had contact with him."

"You might get in trouble. I don't want you losing your job over this." As he merged onto the 10, he cranked his head toward her. "Lincoln or closer to Ocean? I'm not sure how to get to the canals."

"Take Lincoln, and I'll guide you in from there."

As he took the exit, Cade's gaze shifted to his side mirror. He'd been watching his back ever since they left Summer's place. If Lori's first instinct was right, someone just might be following them.

"Are you sure you're safe in this place?"

"Why wouldn't I be?" She lifted her shoulders. "The Player, Clive Stewart, is dead and so are all his copycats."

"I'm talking about the area. Venice has always been sketchy. A cluster of multimillion-dollar homes sitting on the canals doesn't change that."

"When Kyra took possession of the house, she installed a security system—cameras and sensors." She patted his thigh. "I'm safe there."

Lori directed him to a parking lot outside the canal area, and they walked past several homeless people to reach the entrance to the canals. An invisible barrier seemed to exist between the sidewalk and the path into the canals, which the riffraff of the street didn't cross.

The Venice Canals did attract a wealthy bunch because of the proximity to the beach and the home prices, but they tended to be a more artsy crowd than you'd find in Beverly Hills. Hardly seemed a suitable locale for a retired cop.

He followed her across a wooden bridge, where the brackish water slapped against the man-made barrier, the scent of salt permeating the air. A drop of rain splashed near his mouth and he licked it off with his tongue, tasting the salt that already clung to his skin from the night air.

Lori stopped in front of a red door, and Cade glanced up at the camera peeking from the eaves at the corner of the house. She hadn't been kidding.

When she unlocked the door, she pushed it open and stepped inside first. "C'mon in. Excuse the sparseness."

His gaze swept the room. She wasn't kidding about this, either. A couch faced a flat-screen TV, a small end table its only companion. A square table, with two chairs facing each other, hunched next to a sliding glass door.

"Planning to have a dance here later? Is that why you cleared the floor?"

She pushed him into the room. "Very funny. Kyra cleared the old furniture out of the house—too many memories, and I figured this was a temporary solution for me, so I didn't move all my stuff here."

He held up his hands. "No need to explain to me. It's a great spot."

"And the security? Did you check that out?" She pointed to the cameras in the corner of the room. "Kyra even installed them inside."

"You have access to the footage on your phone?"

"Yes." She tossed her purse onto the table next to the couch. "You think I need it now after the job on my tires?"

"Maybe. I'm not saying it was someone sending a warning to Danny in prison and I'm not ruling out someone watching Summer's house, but I think we both know that wasn't a random act. Yours was the only car hit and the vandal got all four tires."

"Funny thing about that so-called warning. If they meant to put me off looking further into Summer's disappearance, the slashed tires had the opposite effect." She leveled a gaze at him from her big brown eyes. "You?"

"Same. I'm all in." Cade rubbed his hands together. "Let's get dinner."

"Would you be crushed if we ordered in pizza? I'm tired and stressed out…and I want to look into Brighter Days."

Cade blew out a breath. For a second, he'd thought she intended to send him home. Pizza in seemed like a reprieve. "You go do what you need to do to decompress. I'll order the pizza. Preference?"

"There's a magnet on the fridge for a pizza place on Washington that delivers. I won't be long."

When Lori disappeared down the hallway, Cade plucked the card for Mario's from the fridge, ordered a large pizza with everything, and a salad, and unearthed an unopened bottle of red wine from the small cupboard above the fridge.

When Lori emerged from the back room in a pair of tight faded jeans and a white T-shirt, Cade held up the bottle and one glass of ruby-red wine. "I hope you weren't saving this for a special occasion."

She drew closer and squinted at the label. "I didn't even realize I had that bottle. Let's kill it."

"Whoa. You *are* stressed out." He handed the glass to her and poured another for himself. "Pizza with the works and a Caesar salad. Will that do?"

"Sounds perfect." Holding her wine in one hand, she slid her laptop from the counter with her other and placed it on the small butcher-block kitchen table. "Wanna help me research Brighter Days?"

"I thought you were stressed out." He swirled the liquid in his glass and took a swig.

"Yeah, and one way to relieve that stress is by solving a few puzzles."

He could think of better ways of relieving stress. In fact, hadn't been able to think of anything else since she sashayed in here with those jeans hugging her backside, but if anything were to happen between them, any old flames rekindling, she'd have to be the one to light the match.

In the end, he'd left her to go away to college, but as he considered their breakup over the years, he'd come to the conclusion that she'd engineered the entire thing. They could've had a long-distance romance, but she dropped off the face of the earth when he went back East.

He yanked out the other chair from the table and swung it beside her. "Let's see if Brighter Days has any answers. Where did you say it was located?"

"There are a few outpatient clinics here and there, but the rehab center is in Topanga Canyon."

He tapped the side of his glass. "That tells you a lot about the place, right there."

"Such as?" Lori's fingers flew over the keyboard.

"Such as, Topanga is stuck in the '60s, so Brighter Days is probably one of those New Age, hippie places that allows you to do rehab at your own pace, in your own way." He took another pull from his glass. "Which explains what Summer was doing there."

"If she did go there for treatment. Maybe she just knows this guy…" Lori propped up the card they'd found in the safe deposit box on her laptop. "Reed Dufrain."

Cade looked over her shoulder as she entered the name of the center, followed by *Topanga Canyon*, in a search engine. Several hits came back; Lori clicked on the official website for Brighter Days Recovery Center.

As she scrolled through pictures of wooded paths, plates of fresh, organically sourced food, exercise rooms, hot tubs and a full-service spa, she whistled.

"I'd pretend an addiction just to go there and relax. Maybe if Danny had had access to a place like this, he never would've continued his drug use and…"

"It's high-end, for sure." He jabbed his finger at the button labeled Staff. "Click this."

The thin face of a bearded man with close-cropped hair filled the screen. Lori said, "This is the center's director, Reed Dufrain. He looks the part, I guess."

"Yeah, like a typical guru." Cade scanned through Dufrain's bio, and the guy checked all the boxes of someone you'd expect in this kind of role at this kind of place. "Oh, hello."

"What?" Lori's finger hovered over the mouse.

"This is a center for women only." He circled an area of the page with his finger and read aloud. "'The center deals with the types of trauma particular to women who abuse substances, creating a safe and nonjudgmental environment.' Yeah, Summer would love that—no judgments."

"Did Summer suffer any traumas?" Lori sipped her wine, and then stared into the glass as the liquid shimmered in the low light of the computer monitor.

"If you count privilege and a surplus of clothes as trauma." He rolled his eyes, his next comment about Summer dying on his lips as he felt Lori's piercing gaze on his face. "What?"

"Talk about judgmental." She clicked on a button for photos. "The fact is, you don't really know, do you? You can never know what someone else is going through, unless they tell you or you see it with your own eyes."

"You're right. Besides, we both know my dad was a control freak who allowed his drinking to control his moods." He let the discussion die between them.

He might be too judgmental of Summer and her choices, he'd admit that, but Lori gave Danny free rein for his choices. Maybe her brother had gotten a bum rap, but she had never faulted him for hanging with the wrong crowd or getting into fights with his girlfriend or being in possession of a stolen handgun.

At least, he'd never heard an ill word of Danny drop from her lips—ever—and he never had the heart to challenge her.

She clicked through the pictures of the wooded grounds and of some gatherings—tai chi, yoga sessions, campfires. Some of the faces of the residents were blurred out and plenty of the shots didn't show close-ups, or captured only the backs of heads, but a few brave souls must've allowed themselves to be photographed for the website. Cade studied the smiling faces for his sister's image.

Lori moved the cursor to the next thumbnail photo and froze, her body jerking beside him. "Oh, my God. Here's our link."

Cade leaned in to study the women stretched out in a yoga class, none with Summer's distinctive blond hair, and said, "What do you see?"

"Her." Lori positioned the cursor beneath the head of a limber brunette. "That's the other missing girl. That's Courtney."

Chapter Seven

Cade's eye twitched as he zeroed in on the woman in the photo. "You're sure?"

"Absolutely. I saw the picture her friend Trey gave the department. We have to tell Detective Marino about this connection between Summer and Courtney. It has to mean something. That's detective work 101—find a link between the victims."

"Wait." Cade grabbed Lori's wrist. "How are you going to explain that you knew about Summer's association with Brighter Days without admitting we ransacked her place and plundered her safe deposit box?"

She raised one eyebrow in his direction. "Ransacked and plundered? We're not pirates. You're a concerned brother who looked through his sister's place to see if he could find any clues to her whereabouts. We don't even have to tell Marino about the safe deposit box. Summer had a card in her nightstand, too. We can give him the card from the bank with the names on it, and tell him we found it in the drawer of her bedside table."

"And the website?" He tipped his chin at the computer monitor. "How are you going to explain finding Courtney on the website? I've never seen a picture of Courtney."

Sighing, she folded her arms and leaned back in her chair. "Do you think it's not allowed for family members to do a little digging on their own? You saw the card for Brighter Days, wondered if Summer had been going there and looked it up on the internet. I was with you and noticed Courtney's picture."

"I'm not concerned about how it's going to look for *me*." He swept her bangs from her eyes with one finger. "I'm worried about you."

Her eyes widened for a second, and she jumped at the sound of a knock on the door. "It's okay. I'm your…friend, and I was with you when you brought up the Brighter Days website. I'm going to get that pizza."

As she started to rise, he put a hand on her shoulder. "I'll answer the door."

By the time he paid the delivery guy and returned to the kitchen with an armful of food, Lori had taken some dishes from the cupboard and topped up their wineglasses. If he finished off that bottle, he'd have a good excuse for not driving home and spending the night here—offering to sleep on the couch, of course. She didn't have to know he usually limited his alcohol consumption to a few beers.

The slashing of her tires had left him with a tight ball of anxiety in the pit of his stomach. Whether connected to Summer's disappearance or Danny's incarceration, the destructive act was a direct threat to Lori.

He took a swig of wine, and then plopped a couple pieces of pizza onto the two plates Lori had placed on the counter. He held up the plates. "Kitchen table?"

"I don't even have a coffee table, so we'd have to balance everything on our knees if we wanted to eat in the living room." She finished scooping the salad into the bowls and grabbed some forks. "Meet you there."

He let her lead the way, the two steps to the table next to the sliding doors, and pulled out her chair. "I'll get our wine."

Cade took a long sip from his own glass before he set them both down on the table.

Eyeing his glass, Lori said, "You'd better slow down if you hope to drive back to your hotel tonight without getting pulled over."

"Maybe I should stay here tonight."

Lori choked on the bite of salad she'd just forked into her mouth. "Not as subtle as you were back in high school."

"I meant I could camp out on that uncomfortable-looking couch tonight in case there's more trouble." He could feel the heat burning in his chest and he fought to keep it from rising to his face by taking a gulp of water.

"I'll be fine, Cade. When I started working at the department, I bought a gun. One of the officers at the station took me to the range to teach me how to shoot." She formed her fingers into a gun and blew on the tip. "I'm pretty good, too, good enough to point and shoot at someone coming through my bedroom window at night."

He swallowed a bigger chunk of pizza than he'd planned and coughed. "You keep it beside your bed, loaded?"

"Doesn't do much good unloaded." She waved her fingers at him. "Don't worry. I'm not going to mistake you for an intruder if you decide to creep into my bedroom."

He snorted. "I have no intention of sneaking into your bedroom in the middle of the night, but if I did, how are you so sure you wouldn't have me pegged as a housebreaker and pull the trigger?"

"Because I'd recognize your...body anywhere." She waved a piece of pizza at him. "I knew that was you at the front desk of the station immediately."

"I'm glad you did." Her teasing banter emboldened him, and he took her hand. "Thanks for your help in this. If not for you, I'd probably be on my way back to New York, none the wiser about Summer, waiting for...something."

She curled her fingers around his hand and squeezed. "I learned my lesson about sitting back and doing nothing. If I had fought harder for my brother when I learned about that unidentified print at the scene of Elena's murder, got him a different attorney…something, Danny might not be sitting in prison right now."

"You were young. There wasn't much you could do." He clasped her hand in both of his, and she didn't even seem to mind the pizza grease. "I hope you're not sitting around blaming yourself for that."

Hunching forward, she said, "Do you think being young is an excuse for making bad choices?"

"Excuse? I don't know if I'd use that word—more like an explanation. We all make bad choices based on our youth. Some people keep on making those bad choices even when they grow up. Look at Summer."

"Summer has an addiction. I don't know if it's much of a choice, at this point." She disentangled her hands from his and wiped them on a napkin.

"At this point, but at another point she had a choice." He tossed back the rest of his wine. "But that doesn't mean she deserves to be missing, and that's what I'm afraid the cops will think once they learn about Brighter Days. Is that Detective Marino just going to dismiss her disappearance as drug related?"

"Not sure." She shrugged and resumed eating her pizza. "That's why I wish the case had gone to Detective Falco instead of Marino. Marino's old-school and more apt to take that view. Falco's new and a woman. She might have a different attitude."

"But you're sure we should tell this Marino about finding the card and seeing Courtney's picture on the Brighter Days website."

"They have nothing right now. That will give them

a place to start, but I still think we contact Trey Ferrar on our own. It could be days before Marino gets around to checking with Trey about Courtney's association with Brighter Days. We can get to the bottom of it faster." She held up the almost empty bottle of wine. "Do you want the rest?"

"Only if you reserve the couch for me." He drummed his fingers on the side of the glass.

"I'll do you one better." She dumped the rest of the wine into his glass, where it sloshed up the sides. "This is a three-bedroom house, and I actually have a bed in one of the other rooms. It's all yours."

"I'll take it, and I promise—" he drew a cross over his heart "—no creeping around in the middle of the night."

"Okay, but you really don't have to worry about me at this house on my own. I showed you the security system, and I have my own backup. I'm fine here."

"A retired LAPD homicide detective was murdered in this house last year."

"He didn't have cameras."

"I'm sure he had a loaded gun on his bedside table."

"He did, but he knew his killer. He let him in and didn't suspect a thing."

He held up his empty glass. "Too late now, anyway. I'm not going to drive home when I'm probably over the legal limit."

"Very convenient. Never saw you down wine like that before."

"Wine?" He collected their plates and bowls from the table. "When we were sneaking booze in high school, we weren't raiding our parents' wine cellars."

"*Your* parents' wine cellar. My parents didn't have a wine cellar."

He huffed out a breath. "You know what I mean. We were drinking cheap beer, when we could get it. I don't think I ever saw you drink wine. In fact, you didn't drink much beer in high school, either. Always the good girl."

"In some ways." She took the dishes from him and spun around toward the kitchen.

He decided to keep his mouth shut. Talking about their steamy sessions in the backseat of his BMW could only lead to trouble. She'd been keeping him at arm's length, and he didn't want to push things or take advantage. She'd helped him polish off that bottle of wine, and the alcohol had brought a flush to her cheeks and a brightness to her eyes that signaled she wasn't altogether sober.

He came up behind her at the sink, placing his hands at her waist. "I'll clean up."

She set the dishes in the sink and cranked on the water. "You do that and I'll call Trey."

"You don't waste any time." He squeezed in next to her and ran the first plate under the water.

"I'll tell Marino tomorrow at work about the connection to Brighter Days. I'm sure he won't get around to contacting Trey for a while. Courtney's case is no homicide."

"Yet." Cade scrubbed at the plate so hard, it didn't need the dishwasher.

Lori rubbed his back. "Don't think like that. It's a good thing Marino doesn't feel any urgency right now. It means he believes the women aren't in any immediate danger."

"They're both gone without a word to anyone. I'm no cop, but that has danger written all over it."

"Cops have to work within certain restrictions. If they tracked down all adults who decided they wanted a break from everyday life, there wouldn't be enough man power to do it—not to mention infringing on people's privacy rights. We do have the right to disappear if we want to." She stepped away from the sink and snatched her phone from the counter. "I'm going to place that call to Trey before it gets too late."

She rummaged through her briefcase from work while he loaded the dishes in the dishwasher, wrapped up the remaining pizza and wiped down the sink.

Perching on one of the stools at the counter, she said, "I'll put him on speakerphone."

Cade sipped from a glass of water, as Lori placed the call. She positioned the phone on the counter between them. It rang twice before a male voice answered.

"Hello?"

"Trey, this is Lori Del Valle. I printed you at the police station as part of the investigation into Courtney's disappearance."

Trey sucked in a quick breath. "Have you found her?"

"N-no. I'm not a cop. I'm calling because I have a personal connection to Courtney's case, and I want to ask you a couple of questions—and share some information with you."

"I don't get it." Trey sniffed. "You know Courtney or something?"

"No." Lori met Cade's gaze over the phone. "You're on speakerphone and my friend Cade is with me. His sister disappeared, too. Do you know someone named Summer Larson?"

"Summer?" He clicked his tongue. "No. I would've remembered that name."

Cade spoke up. "Trey, this is Cade. Did Courtney ever mention a Summer?"

"No. How are they connected? You said you had a personal connection to Courtney. Did Summer know Court?"

"Trey, I'm going to tell you something that we discovered, but you can't tell anyone else that I told you. Don't mention it to the police." Lori braced her hands on the counter, on either side of the phone. "The bloody fingerprint we found at Courtney's place belongs to Summer."

Trey gasped. "Are you saying Summer had something to do with Court's disappearance?"

Cade's hand curled into a fist. "No. My sister is missing, too, but it might mean someone took the two women at the same time. There was a fingerprint in blood at my sister's house, too."

"This is unbelievable. How come the police

haven't called me about that yet? Why haven't they told me about the print?"

"Trey, the police don't have to tell you anything about the investigation. They will probably ask you if you or Courtney knows Summer Larson, but they may not tell you why they're asking the question. That's where we come in. We can do a little extra while the cops have to cross their t's and dot their i's."

"Okay, I get it and I appreciate it because the cops won't tell me anything right now, but I've never heard of Summer before this, so I'm not sure I can be of any help."

Cade cleared his throat. "What about Brighter Days Recovery Center?"

Dead air answered them, and Lori picked up the phone from the counter. "Trey? Are you still there?"

"W-why are you asking me about Brighter Days? What do they have to do with any of this?"

Raising his eyebrows at Lori, Cade answered, "We found a card for the center among my sister's things at her house. My sister was, had been…she's had substance abuse problems, so I wasn't surprised to find the card. I mean, I thought she was clean and sober and had been for a while, so I was disappointed to see the card but not surprised. What about Courtney? Is that someplace she would've known about?"

Trey lowered his voice to a harsh whisper. "I'm not talking about Brighter Days over the phone. If you want to know more, meet me tomorrow."

Chapter Eight

After they arranged with Trey to meet up tomorrow, Lori ended the call and cupped the phone in her hands. "That was weird, wasn't it? The minute you mentioned Brighter Days, Trey clammed up, wouldn't say another word and demanded that we meet in person to continue the conversation."

"Definitely weird." Cade ran a thumb through the condensation on the outside of his water glass. "He almost sounded...scared. Or was that just my interpretation of his creepy whisper?"

"Nope." She tapped the corner of the phone on the counter. "Maybe Courtney was an addict, and he doesn't want to talk about it over the phone. Does that make sense?"

"I guess." He shrugged. "At least he wants to meet with us. Maybe he can tell us something about Brighter Days that'll help the police. Wonder why he didn't tell the cops about Brighter Days."

"Maybe for the same reason you kept quiet about Summer's issues. You said it yourself. Once the cops know a missing person has had problems with drugs in the past, they jump to conclusions and treat the disappearance differently." She waved her hand at the sink. "Thanks for cleaning up. Don't know if it's the tire slashing, the pizza or the wine, but I'm exhausted."

"Maybe it's the adrenaline, but I'm kind of wired. Then again, I could crash in ten minutes. Don't feel like you have to entertain me. I sort of invited myself over."

"Happy to have you." She finished the thought quickly so he wouldn't get the wrong impression. "I—I don't want you drinking and driving."

"And I don't want you here by yourself after that vandalism on your car."

"I'm sure I'm fine, but I really am tired. There's no TV in the guest bedroom, but you're welcome to watch in here."

"Maybe I'll do that. All I ask is for a toothbrush. Do you have an extra?"

"I use an electric, so I have tons in my closet from my dentist. Take your pick." She pushed away from the counter. "I'll leave you one in the bathroom, along with a towel."

He nodded and put his glass in the sink. "Thanks for helping me out today. You've gone above and beyond."

"What's the point of having a contact at the police station if you don't use it? Wish I'd had one when Danny was arrested and charged with murder." Lori headed down the hallway, needing to put some distance between her and Cade.

She pawed through a basket in the hall closet and grabbed a blue toothbrush, still in the package. Then she tucked a towel under her arm and carried both to the bathroom off the hallway. Thankfully, she had her own off the master suite and wouldn't have to share this one with Cade. It was distracting enough having the man in her house, sleeping in her spare bedroom.

She poked her head around the corner of the living room to find Cade slouched on her couch, clicking through the remote. He looked too comfortable, and she swallowed. "I left some things in the bathroom for you, clean sheets on the bed, even though it's just a queen."

"Thanks. That's fine. What time do you get up for work?" He'd paused the TV on some adventure reality show and twisted his head around to look at her.

"I get up around six, leave around seven. You're welcome to sleep in. I can take an Uber to the station."

"That would be one expensive ride. I want to be on that side of town, anyway. Good night, Lori." He turned back to the TV and restarted the show.

"Night."

She washed her face and brushed her teeth, then slipped into a pair of pajamas. She usually wore much less to bed, but in case there was a fire in the middle of the night, she didn't want Cade getting the wrong idea.

She giggled as she crawled between the sheets. She'd banished him to the guest room. She doubted he had any expectations of making it into her bed tonight...even though she wanted him here.

THE FOLLOWING MORNING, Lori woke up to an unusual smell in her house—breakfast cooking and coffee brewing. She rubbed her eyes and squinted at the illuminated numbers next to her bed. Her alarm hadn't even gone off yet. Cade must still be on New York time.

She turned off her alarm and planted her feet on the area rug next to her bed. She could totally get used to this.

Shuffling into the living room, she sniffed the dark, rich aroma of the coffee. That didn't come from her cupboard. Neither did the bacon sizzling in the pan.

She dug her elbows into the counter and propped up her chin with her hands. "Don't tell me you already went out for groceries this morning?"

"Had to." He jerked his thumb at her fridge. "All you had was some leftover pizza, one egg and a couple of strawberry yogurts. Do you not eat breakfast?"

"Usually I just shovel down some yogurt, but I was kinda looking forward to that cold pizza."

He scooped some scrambled eggs onto a plate next

to two strips of bacon, and placed it on the counter in front of her. "Something different today. Coffee?"

"It's been so long since I used that coffee maker. Did it cough and belch steam when you cranked it up?"

"Not quite." He dipped into her fridge like he owned it. "Cream? Sugar? Sweetener? I don't even know how you take your coffee because you weren't drinking it in high school."

"Started that habit in college." She pointed to the small carton in his hand. "I'll take some cream and one packet of sweetener."

"I'll leave room in your cup for the cream." He poured her some coffee in an LAPD mug and shoved it across the counter. "You didn't steal that cup, did you?"

"It was a gift. I'm not the criminal in the family." She dumped some cream into the dark liquid and watched the vanilla swirls fan out. "Do you cook breakfast for yourself like this every morning?"

"I'm as bad as you are. I run in the morning and have a protein smoothie when I get home, usually gulping it down on my way to the office."

Inhaling the aroma of the coffee, she closed her eyes, imagining Cade's routine in New York. "Do you grab a taxi to work? Take the subway? Walk?"

He took a sip of his own coffee and turned away to dump some more eggs on a plate for himself. "I have a car and driver."

"Must be nice." She stabbed a clump of eggs with

her fork and held it up. "I forgot how the other half lived."

"She says from the kitchen overlooking the Venice Canals." He clinked the plate on the counter, and positioned himself across from her.

"You'd pass out if you knew how much I was paying my friend Kyra in rent. I told you. She's doing me a big favor. She could sell this place for a few mil or rent it out for several thousand a month." She bit off the end of a piece of bacon and waved the rest at him. "I'll be looking for a crappy apartment somewhere once she decides what she wants to do with the house."

"Don't compromise too much. You need to be in a safe area, and despite the real estate prices here in Venice, this is not a safe area."

She sealed her lips, not bothering to argue with him about her safety. It felt kinda good to have someone worry about her. The cops at the station gave her tips and looked out for her sometimes, but it wasn't the same as Cade's level of concern. She'd take it for now—revel in it a little.

"I'll keep that in mind." She blew on her coffee and took another sip. "What are you going to do today while I'm at the station?"

"Finish that work I was going to look at last night…and take you to lunch." As she opened her mouth to protest, he held up his hands. "You're not going to leave me on my own here in the big city, are you?"

"This is LA. You grew up here. I'm sure you have lots of friends, but I'm happy to be your lunch date. I'll want to touch base with you anyway to let you know what Detective Marino says about that card and Brighter Days and the connection to Courtney."

"Are you going to tell him about our meeting with Trey tonight?"

She wiped her greasy fingers on the paper towel Cade had folded next to her plate. "He doesn't need to know about that. I'm sure they'll talk to Trey again about a possible connection between Courtney and Summer and their association with Brighter Days. If we get something useful from Trey, we'll turn it over to Marino."

"Won't he wonder why Trey gave you the information instead of turning it over to the police?"

"You worry too much. Let me handle that side of things. Do you want info about Summer's disappearance now, or do you want to wait a few weeks?" She crumpled the napkin and tossed it onto her empty plate. "I'm going to get ready. Do you want to shower here or...?"

"I'll just brush my teeth and then head back to the hotel after I drop you off."

"You really don't have to go out of your way. I can get a ride to the station this morning."

He swept up her plate. "Hit the shower."

"Thanks for breakfast." She hopped off the stool and rubbed her stomach. "It was yummy."

Over an hour later, Cade pulled up in front of the Northeast Division to drop her off.

Standing outside with her hand on the door, she said, "Now you have to drive all the way back to the Westside, and you don't even have your car and driver with you."

"I love LA traffic. Don't forget about our lunch date, and let me know if you have a problem with your car."

"My treat for lunch." She slammed the car door and hurried into the building.

After reporting to the lab, Lori went in search of Detective Marino, thumbing the Brighter Days card in the pocket of her jacket. She sidled into the area that housed the detectives' desks, and then made a beeline toward Marino's.

She waited until he looked up from his computer. "What is it, Del Valle?"

She plopped down on the chair next to his desk and ignored his raised eyebrows. "I have some information about the Courtney Jessup and Summer Larson missing persons cases."

"You have more information about the prints?"

"N-no." She pulled out the card with its bent corner. "You know Summer Larson's brother is an old friend of mine, and I went with him to his sister's house yesterday. He wanted to have a look around once the cops were done."

"And?" He scooted back in his chair and folded his arms over his paunch.

"He found this." She snapped the card on his desk in front of him.

Shoving a pair of glasses on his nose, he brought the card close to his face. "Brighter Days Recovery Center. Drug rehab?"

"That and other things."

"So, his sister's a druggie? That explains a lot."

Lori clasped her hands in her lap, her nails biting into her flesh. "There's more. We checked out the Brighter Days website and saw a picture of Courtney, so they both have a connection to that treatment center. It's in Topanga."

"They're both druggies."

"Well, that's not really the point, is it? They both have ties to Brighter Days and now they're both missing, with one's prints at the other's place."

Marino's eyes narrowed beneath his heavy brows as he sized her up. "Two drug addicts missing? It kinda is the point, Del Valle."

"I thought…"

The detective cut her off and slipped the card into a file. "Thanks for this. We'll have a look."

Knots tightened in her gut, but if she got angry with Marino now, she'd be fighting a losing battle. "Okay, just thought it was something you should know about."

"Thank you." He tapped the file in a way that made her glad she'd held on to the other Brighter Days card, the one with the names.

She shot up from her chair, a little unsteady on

her feet, and spun away from his desk, almost colliding with Detective McAllister.

"Where are you going in such a hurry?" He stepped back to give her space. "How's the house working out?"

"It's great. Tell Kyra I can move out whenever she makes a decision." Detective McAllister and Kyra had gotten engaged, and Kyra had given up her apartment and her newly acquired house in Venice to live with McAllister in the Hollywood Hills.

"She's busy planning our wedding." He rolled his eyes. "Don't ask. She's in no hurry to deal with the house right now, so settle in."

"Tell her thanks again."

Jake dipped his head, watching Marino saunter out of the room, and lowered his voice. "Problems with Marino?"

"Not at all. A couple of missing persons cases, and I know the brother of one of the women. I had some info for him about my friend's sister, kind of off the record."

"Sometimes that's the best kind of information. Too bad about your friend's sister."

Lori had a strong urge to spill her guts to J-Mac, tell him everything about the two cases, and what she and Cade had discovered, but Detective McAllister wasn't on this case. He broke rules occasionally, but he wouldn't undermine another detective in the department.

"My friend is doing everything he can to help the

police locate his sister. Maybe she'll just show up."
Lori held up her crossed fingers.

"I hope so." McAllister jerked his head to the
side. "I have to grab Captain Fields. Good to see
you, Lori."

Lori marched back to the lab, irritation fizzing
in her veins. She and Cade had it right—digging on
their own might be the only thing to spur on this investigation.

The rest of the morning flew by with no hits from
the national fingerprint database on the prints they'd
collected from Summer's house and no further news
on Courtney or Summer. The only prints they could
identify at Courtney's place, besides her own, were
Trey's…and Summer's bloody print. How did that
happen?

Just because Marino didn't have any more information, he couldn't just let the cases go, could he?
She swallowed as she recalled the LAPD's database
of missing persons. One of the LAPD's own detectives, J-Mac's partner, Billy Crouch, had a sister in
that database.

There were certain things she didn't have to tell
Cade. She'd been so good about keeping his child
from him, what were a few more secrets between
them?

Cade needn't have worried about her car. Later
that morning, the garage delivered it with four new
tires—just around the time Cade texted her about
lunch. He insisted on picking her up, though, and

she touched base with her coworkers in the lab before she left.

As she slid into the passenger seat of his rental,
she asked, "Did you get your work done?"

"Enough. I also did a little more sleuthing. I
checked Summer's social media and contacted several of her friends. Some didn't respond, but a few
got back to me." He lifted his shoulders as he pulled
out of the station's parking lot. "Nothing—or at least
they weren't telling me anything. No new boyfriends,
nobody claimed to know Courtney and they didn't
admit to knowing anything about Brighter Days. Of
course, if they were trying to protect Summer, they
wouldn't want to mention she'd been in a treatment
program. I almost called Brighter Days myself, but
figured we should wait to see what Trey had to say
about it first. He had a strange response when we
mentioned it."

"You're really starting to think like a detective."
She clapped her hands. "I've either corrupted you or
introduced you to a new line of work."

The corner of his mouth quirked. "You already
corrupted me in other ways."

She pinched his thigh and said, "I think you have
that the other way around."

"Ouch." He rubbed his leg. "So, I did good by
waiting?"

"Yeah. Let's see what Trey has to say about Brighter
Days before we blunder in there, asking questions.

I gave the card to Detective Marino, but he seemed underwhelmed."

"Really? I thought that was a good lead. He doesn't have anything else—at least not that we know of." He took a quick glance at her. "I'm sure they follow leads without consulting you first, right?"

"Of course." She tapped on the window. "You can park on the street. The lot gets crowded at lunch."

He jerked the wheel to nab a spot between two large SUVs. "So, Marino might be working on something that you don't know about."

"He could be. He doesn't owe me anything. I have a better working relationship with other detectives—especially the ones who were on The Player task force—and they might've kept me in the loop, but not Marino. Our bad luck the case landed with him. He's old-school, keeps things close to the vest. He'd be more likely to tell you if he had something before he'd tell me."

"I haven't heard a word from him since the so-called investigation started. Apparently, Trey hasn't, either."

"Which might make Trey anxious to talk to us tonight." When Cade parked the car, Lori got out on the sidewalk. They crossed the full parking lot to the sandwich place and squeezed in to a table in the corner.

Cade said, "Let me know what you want, and I'll order for both of us."

Lori scanned the menu board behind the counter and gave Cade her order and two twenties. "I'm paying, remember?"

"Got it." He snatched the bills from her hand and got in line.

Five minutes later, he returned with a soda in each hand, and he took the plastic chair across from her, dwarfing it. He'd always been attractive in that lanky, athletic way, but he'd filled out into a fine-looking man. How was he still on the market?

Tapping her straw on the table to unwrap it, she blurted, "Why are you not taken?"

"Taken?" He jabbed his own straw in the plastic lid of his cup. "What do you mean?"

"Oh, c'mon." She shook the ice in her cup. "You know what I mean. Why aren't you married or engaged or cohabitating?"

"Cohabitating? I have a dog. Does that count?" He tapped on his phone's display and shoved it across the table at her. "Meet Dexter, my golden retriever."

"He's cute. Who's taking care of him?" She cocked her head. He was playing dumb.

"My friend and his wife. They have a kid who's crazy about Dexter, and Dex returns the sentiment."

"You're deflecting. Dexter, as adorable as he is, doesn't count. Where's your own wife…your own kid?" She ducked her head to sip her drink. She was on dangerous ground here for reasons he couldn't even guess.

"Would it be a cop-out to say I've been busy?"

"We're all busy, so yeah. Cop-out. Dating? Dating sites?"

"A little and yes. You?" He aimed his plastic fork at her. "I didn't notice a husband and kids at your place. You don't even have a dog."

"I did. I had to put her to sleep shortly before I moved to Venice." She put her hand over her heart. "So, Dexter? Yeah, he does count."

"Have you tried online dating?"

"I have." She held up a hand in his face. "Are you going to tell me it's dangerous?"

"It can be, but I'm sure you're not taking risks."

The guy at the counter called their number and Cade jumped up to retrieve their order, giving her a few seconds to catch her breath. She'd brought up the subject of dating. Now she wished it would go away.

Dating wasn't easy when you kept comparing every new guy you met to a high school boyfriend you hadn't seen in almost ten years. Who did that?

He set down their plates. "Do you need a refill on your soda?"

"Sure." She handed him her cup, and when he returned, she was ready to steer the conversation away from their dating habits.

"Did you find out anything more from Summer's friends?"

"Not much. They seem like a tight-lipped bunch, even when I mentioned Summer was missing." Cade held his sandwich in front of his face, studying it.

"What?" She dropped her own sandwich.

"Maybe Marino is right. Summer relapsed and she took off for parts unknown. Maybe she knows Courtney from Brighter Days, and they fell off the wagon together. The bloody prints and upended furniture could just be a bender gone wrong."

She circled his wrist with her fingers. "Maybe that's all it is and we'd be happy for it, but you still need to find your sister. Benders can get you in trouble. We're not done with our sleuthing yet. We'll talk to Trey tonight, and then give Brighter Days a call."

A man of action, Cade seemed satisfied with her words and dug into his lunch.

She hoped he and Marino were right…but her instincts told her something different.

Chapter Nine

Later that day when she got home from work, Lori changed into a pair of jeans and some boots. Most of the rain had cleared, washing the air clean with it, but the boots would protect her feet from the damp sidewalks and the errant drops that fell from the gray clouds still skittering across the sky.

She pulled on a light jacket over her T-shirt and crossed the bridge out of the canals to wait for Cade to pick her up in his rental car. Trey Ferrar lived in Hollywood, close to Courtney's place, and they'd agreed to meet him there for his convenience. They were the ones who wanted info from him, so it only seemed fair. He needed to be in the right frame of mind to spill the beans on Brighter Days.

Dropping into the seat beside Cade, she held out her phone. "Did you already put the address for the bar in your phone's GPS, or do you want me to do it?"

"You can do it. Tires okay?"

"Great. Feels like a brand-new car. The guy who

slashed them did me a favor." She tapped the address she'd already saved to her phone and brought up the GPS. "Take Lincoln to the 10, and we can get the Hollywood Freeway that way."

Cade pulled away from the curb. "Did you keep an eye on your rearview mirror on the way home? You don't want the same guy doing you any more favors."

She clenched her teeth to suppress a little shiver creeping down her back. "I did watch my mirrors, and nobody followed me home. I think he…or she… delivered the message with the tires."

"Message sent but not received. You're not backing off."

"What else is this person going to do?" She adjusted her side mirror. "I work for the LAPD. He can't stop the investigation."

"That's the point. There is no real investigation, except ours. Did you find out anything new when you went back to work this afternoon?"

"Nothing." She stashed her phone in the cup holder. "In fact, Marino seemed to make a wide berth every time he saw me. He's the type of guy who resents outside interference—especially from techs."

"What about victims' families?" His hands clenched the steering wheel, and she wanted to make him feel better—but she couldn't.

"Marino doesn't consider Summer a victim, and the information about Brighter Days and her past drug use didn't help matters."

Cade's mouth tightened. "I saw that coming."

She couldn't resist any longer, so she ran her fingers lightly down his corded forearm. "We had to let him know. The police are going to be able to get more information out of Brighter Days than we are."

"You're probably right, but the Larsons still have our connections in this city. Dad even knows Mayor Wexler. Maybe it's time to pull out the big guns and tell my father what's going on." He flashed her a sideways glance. "I know you hate that influence peddling."

"Hey, whatever works to find Summer. If I'd had big guns to use to help Danny, I would've used them."

Lori sealed her lips after that. She suspected Cade thought her defense of Danny was unwarranted—most people did. But most people didn't understand, even her own family. Cade definitely didn't get it.

They'd left an hour to get to the bar, the Frolic Room on Hollywood Boulevard, and needed every minute of it.

As Cade pulled up to a valet at a lot across the street, he said, "Hope he waits for us."

"We're not that late, just a few minutes." Lori checked her cell and ended the navigation.

The parking attendant got her door and she stepped into the chilly night, pulling her jacket around her body. "When is it going to start warming up for spring?"

Cade took the ticket from the valet and shoved it

into his pocket. Slinging his arm around her shoulders, he said, "I'll keep you warm."

He steered her down the sidewalk toward the signal, and they hit the curb just as the green Walk sign flashed, blurring into the neon lights around it.

The Pantages Theatre was dark tonight, its Art Deco facade sporting banners of entertainment on the horizon. The Frolic Room huddled beside it, its lighted yellow sign inviting…adventures.

Lori had never been inside the famous dive bar and had no idea why Trey had chosen it. He must live close by. Maybe he frequented the bar regularly and felt comfortable in its dark environs.

Cade opened the door for her, and she stepped into the crowded space, her eyes adjusting to the low lights. Red bar stools lined the wall, facing a mural, and she tugged on the sleeve of Cade's jacket. "Let's perch there for a minute and I'll see if he's here. If we don't grab those seats now, we'll probably lose them in about ten minutes."

They both sat on the stools, facing outward, and Lori squinted as she took in the seats at the bar. No tables dotted the room—you sat at the bar or along the wall, or stood in the space between the two when it got even more crowded than it was now.

She scanned the crowd for Trey's curly black hair and chubby form. A few guys almost had her out of her seat, but when they turned toward her, she ruled them out.

Sighing, she hitched her elbows on the bar behind

her. "I hope he didn't bolt just because we were a few minutes late."

"Maybe he's later. Do you want a beer or something while we wait?" He gestured toward the bar.

"Not really, but you go ahead."

"I'm good, but we'll probably get hassled for not ordering. I'll get a couple of seltzers or soda water."

As Cade stood up, Lori smacked her purse on his stool. "I'll save your seat and give Trey a call."

Cade took a few steps toward the bar and elbowed his way in while Lori checked the door every time it opened. She pulled out her phone and brought up Trey in her contacts. She tapped his name and listened to the phone ring until it flipped over to his message. "Hey, Trey. We're here at the Frolic, sitting on the stools against the wall. Hope you didn't change your mind."

She ended the call and looked up as Cade returned with a drink in each hand and his mouth twisted into a grimace.

"What's wrong?"

He placed the drinks on the bar and plucked something from his pocket. He held up a cell phone in a tiger-print case and said, "You called?"

"What are you talking about?" She licked her dry lips and took a sip of the soda water, the tart lime bouncing against her teeth.

"This is Trey's phone. When you called, I saw it light up on the bar, displaying your number. I checked to make sure you were on the phone. It's his."

She cranked her head from side to side. "Then, where is he? Who leaves their phone at the bar and walks away?"

"That's what I'm going to find out." Cade charged back to the bar, and she followed, the sweating glass nearly slipping from her hand.

Cade hunched across the bar to get the bartender's attention. "Hey, excuse me. Did you see who left that phone?"

"No, but he or she had better come and get it before I turn it off and stash it behind the bar. It has an annoying ring."

Cade made a half turn, locking eyes with a few patrons. "Anyone else? We're supposed to meet him here."

A longhaired, rocker type held up one ringed finger. "I saw him. Young, baby-faced kid. Latino. Met up with some other dude and they went out the back door."

Lori grabbed Cade's arm. "Let's go. Maybe he was given a warning, like me."

Cade thanked the man, and grabbed Lori's hand, leading her to the back of the bar that had to let out on the alley. He pushed on the silver horizontal door release, and a smattering of raindrops hit Lori's face as she followed him outside.

The darkness enveloped them. The neon lights from the boulevard did not permeate back here, and the light over the back door lay in shards at their feet.

Cade crept forward, and Lori hooked a finger in

his belt loop. When he got past the Dumpster, he swore and stepped back, blocking her view. He made a grab for her as she stumbled out from behind him, but he wasn't fast enough.

Lori covered her mouth and choked back a scream at Trey's body splayed before her, his curls sticky with the blood from the slash across his throat.

Chapter Ten

The morning after Trey's murder, Cade hunched forward, elbows on knees, as he stared through the glass at Lori sitting across from her supervisor. He blamed himself for dragging her into their Nancy Drew investigation. He should've trusted the police to do their jobs and stayed out of it. Now Lori faced a reprimand, or worse.

They'd called 911, turned over Trey's phone and explained to the police that they'd had a meeting set up with Trey to discuss his sister and Trey's friend. They kept Brighter Days out of it—didn't want to make a bad situation worse.

One look at Lori's face told him it *was* worse.

They'd already read him the riot act about interfering in a police investigation and pointed to Trey's dead body as proof of the consequences. Did he and Lori contribute to Trey's death by involving him in their search? Trey already involved himself when he broke into Courtney's place and called the police. When people needed answers, sometimes they took matters into their own hands—but he didn't work for the LAPD.

Cade jumped from his seat when Lori and her supervisor stood up and shook hands.

Lori exited the room first, her dark eyes flashing fire and with it a warning to him to keep quiet. "Meet me downstairs."

He nodded once and jogged downstairs to the lobby of the Northeast Division, where he'd first run into Lori. Too bad it took him this long to reconnect with her. He should've looked her up years ago, despite her tiny footprint on social media.

He paced the floor, rejecting two offers of assistance, before Lori swept down the stairs, her head held high and her shoulders pinned back, her bag hanging from her shoulder. He followed her stiff back outside, and then she spun around.

"I've been suspended from work."

Cade's stomach dropped and he reached out for her, but she shrugged him off. "Because of your side investigation?"

"Because of that…" she dashed a hand across her face "…and Trey's murder."

"They're not blaming you for Trey's death, are they?" Of course, he'd just blamed them himself less than five minutes ago.

"Not exactly, but they cautioned me that this is what happens when civilians take matters into their own hands—I think they were talking more about

Trey than us, but we're painted with the same brush." She twisted her fingers in front of her. "I'm so sorry."

"Sorry? You're sorry for what?"

"We've lost our inside edge, haven't we? I can hardly keep on top of the case for you when I'm not on it."

"Let's go to my car so we can talk." Lori had driven to work herself, and he'd been called into the station for another interview regarding the murder. He happened to run into her in the hallway on her way to the meeting with her supervisor. He knew by the set look on her face that she was facing trouble.

When he slid in behind the wheel, he turned to her. "What does the suspension involve?"

"Suspended with pay for one week and when I come back to work, I'm off any crime scene that has to do with these two cases." She smacked the dashboard with her hand. "Why didn't Trey wait for us? Why did he meet someone in a back alley?"

"What did the cops tell you…before they suspended you?"

She rolled her eyes. "Not much. Cameras at the bar caught Trey talking to a man with a hat pulled over his eyes. He must've had the cameras sussed out because he avoided looking into them directly. He spoke to Trey for a few minutes, and then the two of them walked to the back of the bar. No cameras caught them going out the back door, and none caught the murder itself. They don't know if he was forced or tricked into going with the man, but he did leave his phone at the bar. Maybe he suspected something was going to go down."

Cade scratched his jaw. "What if Trey thought the man was me? Obviously, someone knew about our meeting. Some guy could've pretended to be Summer's brother, telling Trey you were on your way or waiting in the back for privacy. You told him I'd be there, but never told him what I looked like."

Lori pinned her hands between her bouncing knees. "This sounds premeditated. Another warning for us and a deadly one for Trey to back off."

"Look, I'm sorry." He placed a hand on her knee to steady it. "I'm not here a week, and I've messed up your job."

"If I don't have to apologize to you, you don't have to apologize to me. I was all in. You didn't coerce me into anything. In fact, this sleuthing around was my idea. I seem to recall your attempts to stop me."

He snorted. "Yeah, I should've known better. I suppose I'll just keep pestering Detective Marino about my sister, daily. What are you going to do with your free time?"

"Are you kidding?" She jerked her head in his direction. "Free time? Your sister is missing, Courtney is missing and Courtney's best friend was murdered just as he was about to give us some information about Brighter Days. We continue to fight."

Cade braced his hands against the steering wheel. "Loretta, your supervisor just reprimanded and suspended you. Do you want to court more trouble for yourself?"

"Loretta? You sound like my mother." She flicked her bangs from her eyes. "Actually, my supervisor was just doing what he was told to do. He never would've suspended me. Hell, I helped The Player task force get their guy because I chose to buck the rules. My supervisor loves me. It's Marino who pulled those strings."

"And he'll pull them again when he finds out you're still snooping around his case. Don't push him."

She huffed out of her nose. "You act like you don't want to find Summer."

"That's not true. I don't want you digging a hole for yourself. Tell me what to do, and I'll do it. You stay out of it." He brushed a lock of silky hair from her shoulder. "I put my family before you once before, and I won't do it again."

She pursed her lips. "But this is Summer we're talking about. This could be life-or-death. Look, every day of my life I regret not stepping up for Danny, for not fighting harder. I've been trying to rectify that for other people ever since. I'm suspended. What are they gonna do?"

"Fire you." He squeezed her shoulder. "Tell me where to start."

"We start where we left off with Trey—Brighter Days. Give them a call on the up-and-up. Your sister is missing. You know she's a reformed addict, and you found their card in her things. Do they know anything? Last time she was there?"

"It's a rehab center. They're never going to give me that information."

"She's missing. They just might, and they'll have to tell the cops if she was a patient." She bit her bottom lip. "Of course, I'm not gonna know about that."

"I should make the call right now. Put them on Speaker with you in the car."

"Do it. And…" she snapped her fingers "… I have a solution to our other problem."

"What other problem? Seems like we have several about now."

"The loss of our inside track. I'm good friends with one of the other fingerprint techs. I'm sure he'll keep me posted on the cases as much as possible."

Cade held out his hand. "Card?"

Lori fished through her purse in her lap and placed it on his palm. "Don't be confrontational."

"How far do you think I'd get in my work if I were confrontational?" He pinched the card between two fingers of one hand and entered the phone number with the other.

As the phone rang, he rested it on the dashboard. "Hello, Brighter Days Recovery Center. This is Natasha."

"Hello, Natasha. My name is Cade Larson, and I'm wondering if you can help me out."

"We will certainly do our best, Cade. That's what we do here—help people."

"Good, good. My sister Summer Larson is missing, and I found your card among her things." He put on his best persuasive voice. "Before you talk to me about confidentiality, I already know my sister has had substance abuse issues in the past. I've helped her get into several programs over the years…and financed many of her stays. I'm wondering if she checked in with you recently, or perhaps she's there now. It would ease my mind to know she was in good hands like yours."

"Oh, I'm so sorry to hear your sister is missing. Of course, everyone's stay here is confidential. What I can do for you is, if Summer is with us, I can get a message to her that you're worried and looking for her. She can call you. There are no rules about calling out."

Cade met Lori's eyes, and she nodded.

"That would be a great start, Natasha. Let her know I'm concerned and just want to hear from her. Not even mad about the relapse, and I'm proud of her for seeking treatment on her own, this time." Cade gave Natasha his cell phone number and signed off with the promise of a donation if they could put him in touch with Summer.

Lori let out a long breath when he ended the call. "That's a start. If she's there, she'll call you. If she's not there and you hear nothing from her, you call them back. Press a little harder about if she ever was there and when they last saw her."

Cade tapped the edge of his phone against his

chin. "Natasha didn't say whether or not the cops already called them."

"Maybe she doesn't know. Maybe the police call went straight to…" she picked up the card he'd dropped on the console "… Reed Dufrain. My contact on the inside, Josh, can tell me if Marino called Brighter Days."

"I should bypass Natasha and reach out to Dufrain next time myself." He flicked the Brighter Days card in her hand with his fingers. "What are you going to do now?"

She slid the card back into her purse. "I have a week's paid vacation. What do you think I'm going to do? I'm gonna help you find Summer—and I've just gone rogue."

WHEN LORI GOT HOME—by herself—she threw in a load of laundry, cleaned out her fridge and surveyed her security cameras. Trey's death had rattled her more than she'd let on to Cade.

She'd had more experience looking at people who had died violently than Cade had. He'd found a homeless man dead in the park on one of his morning jogs, and one of his coworkers had had a heart attack in the office, but blood and guts? He hadn't seen that before. It affected everyone differently and Cade had been shocked but not freaked out.

She'd seen the blood and guts up front and personal at many crime scenes, but Trey's death hit close to home. He was at the Frolic Room at her behest to meet her and Cade—and he'd wound up dead. Someone had slashed her tires in front of Summer's house the other day. Did she and Trey have the same enemies?

She wished she had gotten him to reveal more about Brighter Days over the phone. Why had he been so frightened to talk to her about the treatment center? What was so scary about a rehab center?

If someone killed Trey to stop him from revealing information about Brighter Days, then Cade didn't stand a chance of getting past Natasha at the front desk. But maybe she did.

She called Josh at the lab, and he picked up on the first ring. "Hey, you're persona non grata right now. I probably shouldn't be talking to you."

"Yeah, except I saved your ass on several occasions, and you sorta owe me."

"Hang on." He came back on the line after a pause. "You caught me at a good time. I'm on a smoke break. Otherwise, I never would've answered your call, but hey, I'd have your back even if you hadn't saved my ass a few times."

"That's why I'm calling you."

"You really did step in it though. A murder? C'mon, I thought you were done with all that nosing around after we found out about Clive being The Player."

"We both talked about Clive being weird. I just happened to see more funny business than you did. This time it's personal, Josh. That missing woman,

Summer Larson, is the sister of an old friend of mine. What am I supposed to do? I'm not going to leave him hanging."

Josh lowered his voice. "Especially with Marino in charge."

"I thought you were outside. You'd better not be expressing those sentiments anywhere near the station. I'm already out for a week. We can't afford you gone, too."

"Don't worry. I have a wife and kids. If I lost this job, Ginny would kill me. But…" he coughed "…if you need me on the sly, I'm your man."

"I know that. I don't need much. Just try to keep me posted on any developments on the two cases—especially prints. Also, I gave Marino some information yesterday about both women having a connection to Brighter Days Recovery Center in Topanga. See if you can find out if Marino contacted them yet."

"I think I can find out through the regular channels—you know, coffee room chitchat, bathroom breaks, smoking sessions."

"Guys gossip about work in the bathroom?"

"I hear some of the most amazing things standing at the urinal."

"Okay, TMI, but anything you can find out about Brighter Days would be great."

"Will do. What are you doing with your time off?"

"Did some laundry and cleaned the fridge. I might start on the closets next."

"Almost makes me feel glad I'm at work. I'll talk to you soon."

She'd been lying about the closets. She hadn't been in this house long enough to build up closet clutter. She trusted Josh as her inside man. She *hadn't* been lying about having his back numerous times.

She jumped when her phone rang again, and then slumped in her chair when she saw Cade's number on the display. "Thought you might be Josh calling me back already."

"You talked to him? He's in?"

"He's going to keep me posted on the cases, and he's going to try to find out if Marino called Brighter Days."

"Is it going to be hard for him to get that information?"

Lori tucked one leg beneath her. "Not really. There are a lot of loose lips around the station. It's probably how Clive Stewart was able to keep abreast of the investigation into his crimes. Any luck with Summer's friends?"

"One got back to me, but she swore Summer wasn't using." He sighed. "But most addicts are liars, so maybe the friend just didn't know."

"If Summer wasn't back on the dope, why'd she have those drugs hidden away in her closet?"

"Didn't you point out earlier that if she were really using drugs, they'd be in a more accessible place? Nightstand? Kitchen cupboard? That's a lot of trouble to go through to get a hit."

Lori rubbed her knuckles across the arm of the couch. "Yeah. But if she's not using, why does she have the card for Brighter Days?"

"Referral for a friend? Someone like Courtney? She could've been a patient there before."

"Nothing from Natasha?"

Cade answered, "Didn't expect her to call back. How are you feeling about your suspension? Is there anything I can do?"

"I know exactly what you can do." Lori sprang up from the couch, her heart rattling her ribcage. "You can come over for dinner. I don't often cook, but I have the rest of the afternoon off."

Cade paused for just a second. "Only if you make your mom's enchiladas."

Lori grinned like an idiot. He'd remembered the Sadie Hawkins dance at school. The girls had to ask the boys and pay for the dance tickets and everything else. She didn't have enough money at the time to take Cade out to eat before the dance, so she made enchiladas for him instead.

"I can do that, but don't expect my mom's Carnitas. Chicken okay?"

"Chicken is *bueno*. I'll bring the *cerveza*."

"Only if you promise not to speak Spanish with your horrible accent."

They agreed on a time, and Lori practically flew out the front door to go grocery shopping, ignoring the little warning voice in her head. She scolded the voice aloud in the car. "It's just dinner. We have to eat."

An hour later while the sauce for the enchiladas was simmering, her phone rang and this time it *was* Josh. "What do you have for me?"

"Not much. The cases don't seem to be high priority for Marino. I think he'd need a dead body across his desk before he'd take action." Josh coughed. "Sorry about that. I know it's your friend's sister we're talking about."

Lori swallowed. "Anything on Brighter Days or Trey Ferrar's murder?"

"I don't think Marino is convinced Trey's murder has anything to do with Courtney Jessup's disappearance."

"You're kidding."

"Wish I were, and Brighter Days seems to be a dead end. Police couldn't get any info over the phone, so they're going to have to schedule a follow-up with a subpoena. No estimate on that."

So, Brighter Days didn't want to cooperate with the police. Cade had no chance of getting a call back.

"You are a regular fount of information, Josh. Had I known, I would've been asking you all this time instead of peering through keyholes and putting my ear to the wall." Lori stirred the bubbling sauce, the chilies making her nose run.

"You lucked out on this one, Del Valle. One of my cop buddies is working the cases with Marino—and he's no fan of the detective's."

"I think I know who you mean, and I won't say another word about her...him."

"Anything else you wanna know?"

"I'll be in touch. I'm actually making dinner right now."

"Enjoy your vacay."

Josh's call hadn't brought good news, but Lori had an idea forming in her head, one that could get them primary access to Brighter Days—one that could be dangerous. She'd just have to convince Cade to go along with the plan—and this dinner was the first step.

There was actually one step before this one. She picked up her phone and called Brighter Days.

Chapter Eleven

When she finished the call, she took the sauce off the stove, poured some in a dish and assembled the enchiladas, burning the tips of her fingers as she rolled up the chicken in the tortillas. She started the rice and made a dash for the shower.

Showered, dressed and made-up, Lori put the finishing touches on the dinner and hit the music on her phone. She liked country, and Cade? She had no idea anymore. She selected a classical playlist and turned it low to swirl in the background.

Cade showed up on time with a six-pack of beer and a big smile on his face.

When she ushered him inside, he said, "I could smell those chilies out on the street. You're going to have every house on this side of the canals stopping by with an excuse."

"Don't forget. The last time I made these for you, I had my mom's help. This time I'm flying solo." She took the six-pack from him. "Want one?"

He slipped two from the carton and followed her

to the kitchen. While she stuck the beer in the fridge, he twisted off the caps. "Glass?"

She answered, "Always tastes better from the bottle."

Cade buzzed around the stove, lifting lids and sniffing the air. "Rice, beans. I'm in heaven."

"Just a warning." She held up her finger. "This isn't as homemade as my mom's."

"Still looks great. I'll set the table." He pulled some plates out of the cupboard and carried them to the table. "How is your mom?"

Lori ladled the beans into a bowl and grabbed a couple of serving spoons. "She's doing okay. She's in Mexico now with my grandmother—her mother."

"Do you think she'll stay there?"

"Not sure. My abuela is ill. When she passes..." she shrugged "...Mom might move back here."

They squeezed past each other, as she headed toward the table and he went back to the kitchen for silverware. "I always liked your mom, but I got the impression she wasn't too impressed with me."

A smile tugged at Lori's lips, as she turned with a hand on her hip. "My mom liked you. She just wanted me to be careful around you—thought you were a little too smooth for a high school boy."

"Me?" Cade slapped his hand against his chest. "You never told her about all my awkwardness."

"That was the problem. I sang your praises so much, she warned me nobody was that perfect."

"She was right about that." Cade held up a handful of forks and knives. "Do we need spoons?"

"Just one for the salsa."

They did a little dance in the kitchen again, as she lifted the steaming pan of enchiladas from the oven with a pair of pot holders. "Let me serve you at the table, so you don't mess up my creation. They might fall apart."

"We're eating them anyway, aren't we?" He pulled out her chair and put her beer next to her plate.

She smacked him with a pot holder. "Just let me do it."

She pulled her phone from her back pocket and placed it on the table. Then she carefully scooped out two of the enchiladas and slid them onto Cade's plate. "There. Now you can pile up the rice and beans any way you like."

Cade arranged his food, and as he dumped some salsa on his plate, he asked, "Did you hear anything else from Josh this afternoon?"

She eked out a little breath. Back to business. Of course, he was here because she was helping him with Summer—and for the food. "I did hear from him. The investigation is moving about as slowly as you'd expect. Marino at least called Brighter Days but got no love. He's going to have to return with a subpoena if he wants any info from Reed Dufrain… but I have another plan."

"That's spicy." Cade fanned his mouth. "But so good. I think you're giving your mother a run for her money in the kitchen, but don't tell her I said that. She'd hate me even more."

Lori rolled her shoulders, allowing Cade to change the subject. She should probably wait until after dinner, when his stomach was full and the alcohol had relaxed him. "I'm glad you like it, but my mother doesn't hate you."

In fact, her mother had more blame for her than she did for Cade for what had happened between them and had scolded her for not telling him about the pregnancy.

Mentioning her mother again set them off on a conversation of reminiscing, a conversation they hadn't had yet. A conversation that slightly terrified Lori.

But an hour later, after eating and talking and drinking another beer, Lori couldn't have asked for a better evening. Cade hadn't changed much.

He still took care of people, but his attitude had matured into one of patience and acceptance. She believed him now when he said he had no judgment for Summer's problems.

They'd both had that in common when they were younger—a desire to fix others. She'd done so at the expense of her own well-being, and Cade had let that quality turn him into someone demanding and critical.

As an adult, he'd tempered his desire to help with a greater understanding of others' weaknesses and faults. At the end of high school, she could've told *this* Cade about the pregnancy.

"What?" She stopped scraping the foil label from her bottle when she realized Cade had spoken to her.

"I asked if you wanted another beer." He held up his own empty bottle.

"Oh, God, no, but you go ahead."

"I've hit my limit."

She swirled the rest of her beer in the bottom of the bottle. "So, you're not a big drinker?"

"You mean, like my father?"

"I didn't say that."

"But I could tell that's what you were thinking." He lightly tapped the tip of the bottle against his temple. "Seems like my father's addictive personality manifested in Summer but not in me or Sarah. I don't even like Scotch—my dad's particular poison."

"Pretty much the same with our family. Danny's the only one of us who ever had trouble with drugs or alcohol. The rest of us were turned off by Dad's drinking, but Danny went down the same path."

"Funny how that works." He collected their dishes. "You did the cooking, and I'm going to do the cleaning."

"I'll help." She hopped up from her chair and shoved her phone back in her pocket. She didn't want to miss any calls.

"You don't trust me?" He pushed back from the table as if to race her to the kitchen.

"I'm sure you can do it, but I'm also sure you have a cleaning lady. Go on. Tell me you don't have one."

He raised his hand. "Guilty, but that doesn't mean I don't know how to wash a pan or put a dish in the dishwasher. You saw me in action the other night."

As they stood side by side at the sink, Lori's heart stuttered in her chest. Wasn't this what she'd always imagined for the two of them? They might've been the silly dreams of a high school girl, but she'd felt something with Cade back then, despite their differences, and she still felt it today. She'd never been able to let go of him in her heart—maybe because she still held that secret from him. If she released the secret, told him about the baby, would that release her from the silky web she'd spun for herself? The web that tied her to Cade?

His fingers brushed her hand in the warm, soapy water. "Hey, you're someplace far away tonight. Is that place back in high school?"

She turned toward him, and her breast skimmed his arm, making her toes curl into the floor. "You made me travel down memory lane, and now it's going to be hard to come back."

"Do we have to come back?" He lifted a hand from the water and cupped her face, her hair catching the warm droplets from his fingers. "Sometimes I wish you hadn't let me go so easily. It felt like… you didn't want me."

Tears pricked the backs of her eyes and she blinked. "Oh, I did, but…"

"But you didn't want to hold me back while I was in college. Thing is…" he ran his wet thumb across her bottom lip "…I don't think I would've minded. To be held by you was the greatest joy in my life at that time."

That had to be an invitation.

As she wrapped her arms around Cade's waist, Lori asked, "Like this?"

"More like this." He pulled her close, and her head dropped against his chest, where she felt his heart thunder, mimicking her own.

He wedged a finger beneath her chin, tipping her head back. When his lips met hers, she had to hold on to him even tighter as her knees weakened. He kissed like a man now.

His fingers sifted through her hair, as he deepened the kiss. She slid one hand beneath his shirt and ran her knuckles along his smooth, warm back.

He whispered against her mouth. "Do you want this? Do you want me?"

In answer, she fitted her body against his more closely and trailed her fingers across the reddish-gold stubble on his chin. "When could I ever resist you?"

He grabbed her hand and feathered kisses across her fingertips. "We're different, we're older, but this doesn't feel any different to me. It feels like coming home."

Tugging at the hem of his shirt, she batted her eyelashes at him. "Except we have privacy now, and a bed."

"You mean we can't do it on the kitchen counter?" He tucked his fingers into the waistband of her jeans, and butterflies took flight in her belly. "I actually think we may have done that once or twice."

"Then it must've been at your house because our kitchen was too small and too crowded." She curled her hand around the material of his shirt and yanked it. "Why are you still talking? I thought a man your age would have smoother moves."

"You want smooth moves?" In one motion, he took a step back and swept her up in his arms.

She screamed and tucked her legs in to avoid kicking the beer bottles off the counter. Pointing down the hallway, she said, "This way."

When they reached the edge of her bed, she squirmed out of his arms and pulled his shirt over his head. She splayed her hands across his chest, her fingers tracing his muscles. "Mmm."

That one sentiment sent them into a flurry of activity. If she thought their first time as adults would be slow and easy, she'd sorely miscalculated Cade's impatience—and her own.

With lightning speed, they helped each other out of their clothes and left them in a heap by the side of the bed. Skin-to-skin, they sank to the mattress, and Cade pulled her into his lap. She straddled his hips and gave herself up to the kisses he rained upon her face and throat.

She moved against his erection, and he caught his breath as a shudder went through his frame.

Through gritted teeth, he said, "You're making me feel like I'm eighteen years old again, with no control."

"Control is overrated." She nibbled on his ear, and he swung her onto her back.

One thought pierced the fog of desire that had infused her body. What was she doing? They lived on opposite coasts. Were his actions tonight fueled by guilt or regret?

Then he tucked his hands beneath her bottom and lifted her hips to meet him…and those questions dissolved into a haze of pleasure. She didn't care. She'd take this moment.

Once they'd spent their youthful enthusiasm, they lay next to each other, their limbs entwined. She drew shapes on his damp chest with her fingertip. "I'd say that was an improvement over the previous version."

He rolled his head to the side and kissed her shoulder. "That was just an appetizer—a prelude, a test run."

She did an exaggerated gulp. "You mean there's more to come?"

Running a hand along her hip, he growled. "I feel invigorated. You?"

"I feel…" Her phone rang from somewhere on the floor. "Annoyed."

"I'll get it." He reached to the floor and dragged her jeans up the bed. "You left it in your pocket."

As he removed it, he glanced at the display. "Brighter Days? Why is Brighter Days calling you?"

She snatched the phone from his hand. "Because I'm going to be one of their patients."

Chapter Twelve

Cade tried to grab the phone back from her, but she rolled away from him and answered it.

"Hello?"

Lori had at least put the phone on Speaker, and a familiar woman's voice responded. "Is this Loretta Garcia?"

"Yes, it is. This is Brighter Days?"

"It is. This is Natasha. We got your voice mail, and I'm sorry nobody was here to take your call. Are you safe now? Are you in a good place? We do have emergency services, as well, if you're not."

Lori fluffed a couple of pillows behind her and winked at him. "Yes, I'm fine. As I said in my message, I'm clean right now but I'm in danger of a relapse. I just know it. I've done this before, and I'm going to stop it before it starts this time. Someone referred me to your center, but she doesn't want me to use her name."

Natasha cooed. "Of course. We understand. We

pride ourselves on being discreet. When would you like to come for a visit and discuss your options?"

Cade nudged Lori's knee and sliced a finger across his throat when her eyes met his. She was *not* doing this. After Trey's reaction to the place and his murder, Cade didn't want Lori anywhere near Brighter Days.

She gave him the okay sign with her thumb and forefinger. "How about tomorrow?"

Cade dragged his fingers through his hair, grasping at the roots. How long had she been planning this?

"Tomorrow is fine. We can see you at eleven o'clock, if that's okay. Do you need directions?"

"Eleven is fine, and I have the address in Topanga. C-can I bring my friend with me?" She leveled a finger at him. "If I decide your center is right for me, he'll be making the deposit for my stay—in cash."

Cade let out a breath. At least he'd have the drive over to talk her out of it.

Natasha answered brightly, "Of course, but he can't take the tour—anonymity and all that. The road to our facility is a windy one, once you turn off Topanga Canyon Boulevard. Keep following it all the way to the end and you can park on the right and use that entrance."

"Thank you, Natasha."

"We'll be waiting for you, Loretta."

When Lori ended the call, she held up her hand. "Don't start. You know this is a good plan. What are we going to do, wait for Marino's subpoena? What's he going to find there?"

"What do you think *you're* going to find? Trey told us he wanted to talk about Brighter Days in person, and before he could, he was murdered. This is a dangerous move, *Loretta Garcia.*"

"It'll be fine. I'll check in as an inpatient, go to a few therapy sessions, do a little yoga—and snoop around in my spare time."

He punched his fist into a pillow. "That's what I'm worried about. What if someone catches you nosing around? Do you have a story?"

"I'll think of something." She flicked her fingers in the air. "I'm not going to do anything stupid, Cade. I just want a firsthand look at what goes on in there. Maybe I can chat up a few of the patients and see if anyone knows anything about Summer or Courtney."

"That right there is gonna get you kicked out…or worse." He swung his legs off the side of the bed and planted them on the floor. "When were you going to tell me about this? I mean, I do have to finance the scheme."

"I tried to tell you earlier, before dinner." She slid him a gaze from the side of her eye. "But I didn't want to ruin your dinner."

"Or you just wanted to get me drunk and…" he plucked up the sheet and let it drop "…sated."

She curled up her leg and wiggled her toes against his bare back. "Are you sated? You just told me five minutes ago we'd only gotten started."

"That was before I knew you'd committed your-self…and my money to Brighter Days."

She got on her knees and pressed her breasts against his back, as she wrapped her arms around him. "You're still going to finance me, aren't you? I can pay you back, but I figured you'd have a bet-ter chance of getting your hands on bundles of cash than I would on such short notice."

He took her hand that rested on his shoulder and turned it over, placing a kiss on the palm. "I'll give you the money if you promise we'll put a plan in place in case you run into something you can't han-dle."

"We will." She leaned forward to kiss the edge of his chin, the ends of her hair tickling his skin. Then she whispered in his ear. "Can we take it slow and easy this time?"

Cade tumbled back onto the bed, taking her with him. He still hadn't given up on convincing her to abandon this wild scheme, but he'd save reason and sanity for the light of day.

THE FOLLOWING DAY, Cade walked out of his bank, the same one that housed Summer's safe deposit box, carrying a stack of cash in his computer bag. As he tossed the bag in the backseat, he asked Lori, "How much time is that going to buy you?"

"That'll be a deposit on one month's stay." She slammed the car door. "And if I leave early, which I will, you'll get that refunded."

"Unless you discover you like it there and wanna see out your month."

She punched his biceps. "I highly doubt I'll like it there. Sounds like a bore, but I'm hoping to get some insight into why Trey was leery of this place."

"Leery? Trey sounded more than leery." He wagged his finger at her. "Don't forget Trey is dead. The cops have no leads, except for some video of the back of the killer's head and the bartender's vague recollection of his face. *And* someone slashed your tires after you found the Brighter Days card at Summer's house and again in her safe deposit box."

"The perps who slashed my tires didn't know I found those cards."

"They figured you were going to find something they wanted to keep a secret, and that something might be Summer's connection to Brighter Days." He started the car and trailed a finger down her soft cheek. "Just remember that you may be in enemy territory while you're there."

She held up two fingers like a Boy Scout. "I'll remember. Now, we need to find you a disguise before we drive out there."

He slammed on the brakes, and they both lurched forward against their seat belts. "Excuse me?"

"Disguise. You'll need one. Both you and Summer have those blond-blue, California-gold good looks. Someone might recognize you. Maybe they already did some research on Summer and saw your picture.

I've gotten this far, and I'm not going to jeopardize my cover."

"Your cover?" He snorted and continued to pull the car out of the parking space. "Okay, Loretta Garcia."

"I'm not searchable on the internet, like you are. My parents aren't international businesspeople and philanthropists—unless you count the church collection plate. Garcia is a common name, if they do decide to investigate me. They're going to be inundated with Loretta Garcias if they try. Besides…" she straightened her seat belt "…I'm going to alter my appearance, too."

He raised his eyebrows and rubbed her thigh. "Not too much. I like what I see right now."

"Nothing drastic." She flipped down the visor and studied herself in the mirror. "Maybe some glasses, more and different makeup and a wig."

"Wig?" Cade laughed. "You're serious."

"Do you want me to be careful, or not? If I'm already on their radar for some reason, I want to go there incognito."

"Okay, you're right. Disguise it is. Where are we going to find these disguises?"

"We're a few miles away from Hollywood. If you can't locate a costume shop here, you don't belong in Tinseltown." She pulled out her phone and tapped the display. "Found one or two."

Lori pulled up one of the stores on her GPS, and Cade followed the directions.

When they got to the Hollywood Costume Shop

on Sunset, Elsa the salesperson didn't blink an eye as they shopped wigs, beards, colored contact lenses and hats.

As Cade patted the dark beard on his face, he asked her, "Do you do a lot of business?"

"This is Hollywood. People change their identities all the time." Elsa peered at him over the top of her glasses perched on the end of her nose. "You look good with a beard."

Lori turned from the mirror, a short curly wig covering her silky tresses. "What do you think?"

Picking up a hat, Cade said, "I think I like the previous version better."

"I hope so, but do I look different enough?" She pulled the hair back from her face. "Too recognizable?"

Elsa tapped her chin with one long red fingernail that matched the color of her hair. Or maybe that wasn't her hair.

She considered Lori's face. "Put on some makeup. You can go dark with the black hair. I can show you a few contouring tricks that will change the shape of your face. Throw on some glasses, and you'll look very different from the woman who walked into this store. Different enough so that even your husband won't recognize you—if that's the plan."

Lori met Cade's eyes and smothered a smile with her hand.

Elsa thought they wanted to spice up their sex lives by changing things up in the bedroom. She couldn't be more wrong—he wouldn't change one thing in the bedroom.

Lori nodded. "That would be great. The extent of my makeup routine comprises some black eyeliner, mascara and a swipe of lipstick when I'm not eating, drinking or talking."

"That's because you're naturally beautiful." Cade came up behind her in the mirror and brushed his new beard against the back of her neck.

She shimmied. "That tickles. Watch out. I may just demand you keep that glued to your face."

Cade swept the baseball cap he'd picked up onto his head, shoved his hands in his pockets and slouched. "I'm going for hipster Hollywood director with too much money to care for fashion—or cleanliness."

Elsa smirked. "Works for me. Now, let me get my brushes."

Thirty minutes later, Elsa had transformed a fresh-faced beauty into a poster child for a "just say no" campaign. Lori stared at him from heavily lined eyes and puckered a set of ruby-red lips at him. The dark hollows beneath her eyes emphasized her cheekbones, which stood out sharply from her face. She could pass for a recovering addict easily.

She spread her arms. "What do you think? Black-on-black clothes, Elsa?"

"Absolutely—black jeans, boots, T-shirt, edgy jacket. You'd fit in at any club on the Strip."

Lori checked her phone. "We're headed somewhere else, but this will do. We'll take everything and wear it out—just to get accustomed to the disguises."

When they landed outside on the sidewalk, Cade ducked every time someone walked by. "I feel like an imposter."

"You are." Lori thumped him on the back. "But if you're going to play the hipster director, you'd better own that persona and stop hunching every time someone looks at you."

"This is exactly why I never did theater arts in school."

"You didn't do theater arts in school because you thought those kids were nerds, and you were the hot-shot athlete."

He tugged on the scratchy beard. "Was I that insufferable?"

"Sometimes, but you were always kind to everyone…even the little Latina from East LA. Once I had your attention, no one ever dared to bully me."

"Nobody was going to bully you anyway. The boys thought you were hot as hell, and the girls saw you as a project."

She drilled him in the back with her knuckle. "Now you're my project, so you'd better play the part—a good, rich friend concerned about his friend relapsing, needing anonymity and putting cash down as a deposit."

"What am I supposed to do while you're taking the tour?"

"Smile and drink your green smoothie."

He said, "Then I'll head to the bathroom, get lost and do a little reconnaissance on my own."

"I wonder if they can take me as soon as tomorrow. I do have to get back to work in a week."

He took her arm and led her to the car parked down the street. "You hope so. If the LAPD finds out about this stunt, you may not have a job to go back to."

AFTER THEY CHANGED into appropriate clothes to match their disguises, Cade drove his rental along the Pacific Coast Highway. As they cruised past Malibu, Lori asked, "Do your parents still own the house?"

His gaze flicked toward the azure sea to his left. He'd spent much of his childhood in that water. He missed it. He'd given up too much in his quest for independence from his father. He shot Lori a look from the side of his eye. Maybe it was time to get it back.

Flexing his fingers on the steering wheel, he answered her. "They still own it. They rent it out. Do you remember where it is?"

"Of course. I'll never forget that house—the ocean views from every room, the pool looking almost seamless with the ocean, that kitchen. How come Summer doesn't stay there?"

He lifted his shoulders. "Too big for her. That's a family home. Too far away from the city and the things she likes to do—the things that got her into trouble."

"At least we're doing something to find her instead of sitting around waiting for Marino."

His stomach dipped just like it did every time he thought of Lori trapped at Brighter Days. What had Trey been so afraid of? Had he paid with his life because of what he knew about the treatment center?

"If we don't like the look of the place or the people running it, all bets are off. I'll take my bag of money and go. This is just a tour. You don't have to commit to anything."

"Okay, we'll see how it goes." She tapped the window. "Topanga Canyon Boulevard is coming up at the next light."

Cade made the turn and maneuvered the car along the winding, two-lane road that cut through canyons and forests. Wildfire season could hit this area hard. He remembered watching a few times from his house in Malibu as an orange haze hung over the mountains here.

He took the turnoff toward Brighter Days, but the facility hadn't bothered to put out a sign. If you needed a sign to find Brighter Days, you didn't belong there. Lori didn't belong there, either.

"This is off the beaten track, isn't it? No wonder they have such great views to show off on the website." She fluffed her black curls and smacked her lips to moisten her lipstick. "Natasha said veer to the right and we'll see parking and an entrance."

Cade rolled past a delivery truck from a high-end natural food grocery chain and spotted a handful of parking spaces. "At least you'll be eating well while you're here—if they don't kick you out first—or worse."

"Stop worrying." She squeezed his arm. "I'm going to make a few discreet inquiries and see if I can access any computers."

He jerked the car to a stop. "Wait, what? You never mentioned computers before."

"How else am I supposed to get any info on patients? Do you think they keep filing cabinets stuffed with patient details?"

"You know about computers, too?" He narrowed his eyes. He could still make out Lori under the disguise. He'd know her anywhere, although he wouldn't have noticed her at the Northeast Division the night that he went in to report Summer missing if she hadn't noticed him first. That night made him believe in luck…or maybe it was fate.

"I'm not a hacker, but I know a little about computers. We have a kick-ass tech guy, Brandon Nguyen, who taught me a few tricks. I can get past a password or two."

"You just heightened my anxiety, tenfold." He cut the engine and took a deep breath. "All right. Let's get this over with. Remember, you can walk away from it all."

"Got it." She winked and cranked open the car door.

They walked up a gravel path that led to a side entrance. A bubbling fountain greeted and soothed them at the door and Cade tried to open it. While his hand still rested on the handle, he heard a muted buzz and a soft click. It turned beneath the pressure of his hand.

As soon as they stepped onto the cool tile of the foyer, an attractive woman with dark hair pulled into a bun floated toward them, hands outstretched. "Loretta, here for the tour?"

"Y-yes. Are you Natasha?" Lori knotted her fingers in front of her, looking as nervous as he felt.

"I am." Natasha reached out and captured Lori's hand with both of hers, expensive-looking rings sparkling on her long fingers. Cade had been around jewelry long enough to know the real thing. The rehab business must be booming.

"And you are?" Natasha turned her dark, inquisitive gaze on Cade in a way that made him want to tug down his cap.

"Her friend."

Natasha threw up her hands. "I get it. Well, friend, I did mention to Loretta on the phone that we give tours only to prospective patients, so you'll have to wait in our lounge while I show her around."

"Understood." The fewer words he said, the better. He didn't think she'd recognize his voice from one phone call, but let her think he was afraid she'd out him as someone famous who didn't want to be seen at a treatment center.

"Good. Then we all understand each other." She

reached past them and pressed a button on the wall. "Ready, Loretta?"

Cade half expected the button to release a trap door, dropping them into the bowels of this bucolic retreat, but it only summoned a short dark woman in some kind of green tunic that looked like a nurse's uniform.

"Ella, please see this gentleman to the lounge and offer him refreshment." Natasha waved her slim hand in the air. "We have smoothies, organic coffee, herbal teas, whatever you like."

Lori made a little move beside him, and he had to clench his teeth to trap his laugh.

"Thanks." He turned toward Ella without another glance at Lori. Some instinct told him Brighter Days preferred clients who didn't have a lot of outside support. He could be wrong, but he didn't think so.

He'd figured that was the reason why Lori had identified him as a friend to Natasha over the phone instead of a husband. A husband or boyfriend could be bothersome. At least, that was his story, and he was sticking to it. It couldn't be that Lori didn't like the idea of calling him Husband.

He followed Ella into a beautiful room with two glass walls, the nature outside clambering all over them to get inside. The room seemed like an extension of the outdoors, and he sank into a teak chair with green floral cushions, facing the riotous growth.

"Can I get you something, sir?"

"How about a green smoothie? Something healthy."

He suppressed a smile. Lori had nailed this place. He just hoped he was wrong about the rest of it and that Brighter Days wasn't complicit in Trey's death. Because where would that leave Lori?

"Of course, sir. Any allergies or restrictions?"

"None. Thanks for asking." They really wanted his money. This just might be the most expensive green smoothie he'd ever had. When Ella left, he glanced at the tables littered with books on meditation, yoga, veganism. He didn't see any informational pamphlets about the center. Business must come via word of mouth among the wealthy and connected.

Mom had spent a month in a place like this for her prescription pill addiction. How Mom and Dad could read Summer the riot act about her drug use was the epitome of irony, given their own addictions. They had to figure they'd turn out one child with issues.

His sister Sarah had different issues—control issues. She left nothing to chance. She even organized her kids' birthday parties down to the last balloon.

Who was he kidding? He'd had the same type of predilections. He'd worked hard to overcome them. His business went smoother when he allowed his top executives to have a say in the direction of the company. So far, so good. He'd outearned his father last year for the first time—not that that was his primary goal.

"Your smoothie, sir." Ella sailed into the room with a tall glass filled with green mush on a silver tray.

She set it in front of him on the table and he unwrapped the straw and stuck it in the sludge. She hovered while he took the first sip. He closed his eyes and said, "Perfect."

"Let me know if you need anything else, sir." Her shoes whispered on the tile, as she left him to his glass of health.

He took another sip and smacked his lips. To break the silence that hung over the room, he said aloud, "Not bad."

They should probably have music. No sooner had the thought left his brain, than some Peruvian flute music floated from the hidden speakers. Maybe they could read minds here, too.

The sound of heels on the tile echoed from the other room and once again, he heard the buzz and the click of the door. Another prospective patient? Did they get their times mixed up? What happened to Brighter Days' famed discretion?

He pushed up from the chair, drink in hand, and wandered to the arched entry to the foyer. Natasha ushered in two men in suits, who didn't look like prospective patients to him.

As the taller guy in the gray suit turned to glance at him, Cade almost choked on his green smoothie.

He knew they weren't prospective patients—because the man in the gray suit was Detective Marino.

Chapter Thirteen

Lori gazed at the view from the patio, staring past the outdoor yoga lesson. The circuitous coastline etched in blue with a white edge twisted its way up to Ventura County, the rugged Santa Monica Mountains almost meeting the sand. She could get used to a place like this.

Cade's childhood home had just such a view, although from a lower elevation. She'd loved that house. The beach off the house's back deck wasn't private, but it was far enough away from public parking and the primo surf spots of Topanga Beach and Surfrider that not many people ventured down to the sand.

She and Cade had made love on that beach— stupid, foolish, teenage sex—not thinking about the consequences.

She jumped when Natasha came up behind her. "I'm sorry, Loretta. I have a few more areas to show you, but I have to deal with a situation right now. I can have Ella continue the tour, if you like."

"I've seen enough, Natasha. It looks like the perfect setting for me. I'm determined to stay clean this time."

"We can certainly help with this first, rough period of sobriety." She slipped a folded piece of paper into Lori's hand. "The payment options. Ella can assist you with the deposit and schedule for your stay."

She was in. "D-do you think I can start tomorrow? I'm on shaky ground right now, and my friend out front, the one financing this, has kind of had it with me. He has work in Canada and will be out of town."

"Tomorrow is fine." Natasha patted her back. "Ella will give you all the details."

She followed Natasha across the patio, back inside the airy building. What possible evil could take place behind the walls of such a place? Maybe she and Cade had it all wrong. Maybe Trey had it all wrong.

They stepped into the lobby area, and Lori nearly tripped to a stop. Positioned by the side door, arms folded over his belly, loomed Detective Marino.

Her knees quaked as they walked past him and his partner, Detective Suarez. Both detectives discreetly averted their eyes from her, as she dropped her head, letting the curls from her wig hide her face.

Natasha left her at the small ornate desk in the corner, clutching its edge, as she turned toward the cops. "Gentlemen, come this way and tell me what you'd like to see."

As the two suits lumbered toward Natasha's office, Lori let out short little breaths and placed her hand against her heart. She cracked her stiff face into a smile when Ella joined her at the desk.

"I'll take care of you, Loretta. You're joining us tomorrow?"

"Yes."

Cade sauntered in, clutching a glass with green residue stuck to the inside. "You're going ahead with it?"

"I am. Now you can go to Canada with a clear conscience. I'll be here." As she faced him, away from Ella, she brushed her fingers across her forehead, indicating she'd had a close call. Had he seen the detectives?

They settled their business with Ella, and Cade handed over the cash for the deposit. He requested a generic receipt for the money, and Ella scurried from the desk, cash in an envelope.

Cade whispered. "Did Marino see you?"

"Yes, but no hint of recognition from him or Suarez. I'm safe." She sealed her lips as Ella emerged from the office, waving a white slip of paper in the air. "Here you are, sir. Do you need anything else?"

"I think we're set." He placed the empty glass on the desk. "And thanks for the delicious smoothie."

Lori waited until they were in the car before turning toward him. "You really ordered a green smoothie?"

"It was good, although I nearly upchucked all of it when I saw Marino walk in. So, he got his subpoena faster than we thought he would. Maybe he's taking this seriously, after all."

"Who knows? Maybe Reed Dufrain decided it would be a better look for him to open his doors to the LAPD than force them to issue that subpoena. They'd have had time to hide whatever needed to be hidden."

He eased the car back onto Topanga Canyon Boulevard and some semblance of civilization. "If there's anything to be hidden. I didn't have a chance to get lost after the detectives showed up. What did you see on the tour? Anything nefarious? Looks like your typical high-end rehab center to me."

"I'll get a better look tomorrow, won't I?" She cracked the window and sniffed the air. "Smells so good up here."

"Do you want to stop by my old house on the way back? I've been handling the rental for my parents, and the tenants indicated they wanted to move out at the end of their lease. I told them I'd drop by on this visit to discuss some terms with them."

"I'd love to see the old house." She grabbed a handful of curls. "Are we going like this?"

Cade chuckled. "I got so comfortable with the beard and dark wig, I forgot I had them on." He tapped his phone sitting in a holder on the dashboard. "I'll call the tenants to see if it's okay that we drop by. The husband works at home. He writes scripts for a few very popular TV shows, and his wife stars on one of the shows. If it's a go, we can stop for lunch at the Reel Inn and shed our costumes."

She tapped her forehead. "Aren't you glad I insisted on them? Marino would've made you in two seconds, and both he and Suarez would've hauled my sorry behind back to the station."

He clicked his tongue. "Your behind is anything but sorry—and I know that for a fact."

She gazed out the window with a stupid smile on her face. She wasn't sure yet how this was all going to work out between them, but she'd enjoy the ride for as long as possible.

She covered her mouth. That didn't mean she was happy Summer had gone missing, and was still missing. She'd have given up running into Cade again if both Summer and Courtney could come home safely. Wouldn't she?

Cade spoke to the man on the other line for a minute or two. The tenant had agreed to meet Cade in an hour.

"Lunch and a change of clothes."

Lori's heart skipped a beat for a second, as she glanced in her side mirror. "Nobody followed us from Brighter Days, right?"

"I've been keeping an eye on the rearview. Kinda hard to tell when you've got a two-lane road most of the way—one end spilling out on the coast highway, the other end onto Ventura Boulevard. But I haven't noticed one car behind us the whole way. Do you want me to pull over for a few minutes in case we have a distant tail?"

"Would you mind? I don't know why it didn't occur to me before. We had the disguises and the cash-only payment, but Natasha could get suspicious and have us followed. Maybe it's even protocol for them."

"Okay, hang on." Cade wheeled the car into a small dirt parking lot in front of a marijuana dispensary. As he backed up to face the road, he said, "I'm sure this store does a booming business up here."

"Charlie Manson stayed in Topanga for a while before relocating to Spahn Movie Ranch due north and across the valley."

"Yeah, don't remind me. That's just another reason for you to abandon this scheme."

"Charlie Manson is dead and gone." She brushed her hands together.

"Plenty more devious minds out there, and we both know Topanga isn't all peace and love." Cade hunched forward over the steering wheel for several minutes, watching the traffic cruise past. "I don't see any familiar cars. I think we're good to go."

He peeled out of the parking lot, kicking up dust and gravel with his back wheels. Several miles later, they stopped at the bottom of the boulevard to make a left turn at the light, an expanse of the Pacific Ocean gleaming in front of them. Less than a mile away, Cade turned onto a street bordering the Reel Inn, a casual seafood restaurant with barrels of peanuts for appetizers and shells on the floor.

As he parked the car, he said, "I can do my quick-change act out here." He pulled down the visor and carefully peeled the beard and moustache from his face, leaving a ruddy color behind on his skin.

He patted his face. "Almost there."

He tossed the baseball cap in the backseat of the car and pulled the dark wig from his head. He tousled his blond hair with one hand. "What do you think?"

She leaned over and kissed his clean-shaven cheek. "Much better. Now, it's my turn."

She removed her own wig and shook out her hair. She'd already ditched her glasses and wiped off the lipstick. "I'll wash my face in the restaurant. This disguise was good enough to fool Marino and Suarez, so that makes me feel better. I just need to re-create that makeup every day at the center."

"Hopefully, you won't be there long enough to perfect it. You're going to have a sudden change of heart or a family emergency once you find what you want, or realize there's nothing there to learn." Cade scratched his beardless face. "If the subpoena doesn't turn up anything, maybe you should cancel. I can eat the deposit."

Squeezing his hard biceps, she said, "Stop trying to talk me out of it. I can uncover things a subpoena can't. Marino and Suarez aren't going to be talking to the patients."

Self-conscious about her heavy makeup, Lori kept

her head down when they entered the restaurant and made a beeline for the restrooms. She'd already given Cade her order and by the time she emerged from the ladies' room fresh-faced and hungry, Cade had snagged a table on the patio and had filled a basket with peanuts.

She slid into her chair and took a gulp of her iced tea. "Better?"

"It's all good to me. You could wear a bag over your head, and I'd be happy to sit across from you. No, wait. The bag would have to have cutouts for your eyes, so that I could gaze into their depths."

She snorted and took another slug of her tea, even though she couldn't quiet her singing heart. "Have you been watching romance movies? You already got into my bed—you can relax now."

He tossed a peanut shell on the ground and grabbed her hand, lacing his fingers through hers. "That's not what it's about between us. It never was. You don't believe that, do you?"

She studied his blue eyes, sparkling with intensity. That intensity made her shy. There was so much between them, so many unspoken words—at least on her part.

She traced the seams where their fingers interlocked. "There was always more, but what now? You live in New York. You're here to find Summer, and I'm helping you. When we find her, and I know we will, you'll go back to your life and I'll go back to mine."

He released her hand and stirred his tea with his straw. "Don't you think there's a reason neither of us is married or even dating exclusively?"

Beyond the reason that she compared every man to her first love? "You thought about me so much over the years, you never once contacted me."

"I can take a hint, Lori. You broke it off with me. You were supposed to join me that summer in Boston before we started college. You were going to look into transferring. Yeah, I know I could've chosen a college in California, but I wasn't strong enough then to stand up to my father. He wanted me to go to Harvard, so that's where I went."

"I didn't blame you for that." She blamed him for not fighting harder for her. She blamed him for not asking more questions. She blamed herself for so many things.

Sweeping some shells to the floor, she said, "It's not about the past anymore. It's the future that concerns me. If I wouldn't move across country then, I'm not going to do it now and I don't expect you to give up your life in New York, and everything you built there."

"I can achieve that kind of success in any big city—even here."

The waiter saved her from answering, as he dropped off their fish tacos and refilled their tea.

When he left, she asked Cade, "Is the first step looking at the Malibu house?"

"Maybe it is."

Despite her doubts, a fish taco never tasted so good.

Forty minutes later, they were cruising down the Pacific Coast Highway once more before turning down a road that led to the ocean and the mansions perched along its coastline.

Cade rolled up to the security gate and buzzed down the window. He waved his hand outside. "They're expecting me, Raoul."

"Nice to see you again, Mr. Cade."

"You, too. How's the family?"

Raoul gave him a thumbs-up and a big smile as he raised the parking arm.

Cade drove onto the small road that curved along the edge of the houses, most of which you couldn't see behind the large gates. He pulled up to the familiar Mediterranean-style house with the red-tile roof and soaring arches. When Lori first saw this house, she thought it was a palace and Cade was surely her Prince Charming.

She swallowed against her dry throat. "Looks the same."

"Feels different." Cade jumped out of the car, and he steered her up the long walkway to the front door, which opened before they could knock.

A tall, lean man with glasses shoved to the top of his head stepped onto the porch. "Saw you coming. How are you doing, Cade?"

Cade introduced her to Jerry Wise, who invited her to relax on the patio while he and Cade discussed business.

As she sauntered toward the pocket door that opened onto the deck and a crisp, salty sea breeze, Jerry asked her if she wanted anything to drink.

"Lemonade, wine, champagne, Bloody Mary. Whatever you like."

"Lemonade is fine."

"Go on out." He shooed her with his bony fingers that she could imagine toiling over a computer keyboard, churning out scripts for hit shows. "I'll have my assistant, Gretchen, bring you a drink."

Lori stood at the railing, leaning over to watch a mom and her two small kids building sandcastles. She turned when she heard scuffling steps behind her.

A young blonde woman with her hair in a chignon held up a tray with a pitcher, a glass of ice and a bowl of tropical fruit. "Jerry said you wanted some lemonade and insisted I include some food. For as skinny as the guy is, he's constantly eating and thinks everyone else should be, too."

"It looks lovely. Thanks." Lori peered at the jug of pale yellow liquid still rippling from a vigorous stirring. "This isn't hard lemonade, is it?"

"No." Gretchen's laugh was like the trill of a bird. "He thinks everyone in Hollywood drinks in the middle of the day, so he always offers alcohol. I can spike it if you like."

"Oh, God, no." Lori grabbed the handle of the glass pitcher before Gretchen could. She didn't know how often this young woman's duties involved serving food and drink to Jerry's guests, but Lori didn't want to waste her time.

The glass tinkled as she filled it. Holding up the pitcher, she asked, "Do you want to join me?"

"Would love to, but I have a Diet Coke at my desk that includes a pile of work."

"Then I won't keep you. I don't need anything else, thanks."

Gretchen tipped her head toward the view. "I'll miss this when the Wises go back to New York."

"You're not going with them?"

Gretchen shook her head so hard, her bun slipped. "I'm an LA girl, born and bred. There's something about this place that seeps into your blood, isn't there?"

"I agree." Lori raised her glass to the ocean and took a sip, the tart lemonade spiking her tongue. She whispered as Gretchen turned away, "Especially when you have this view."

As she drained her second glass of lemonade, Cade and Jerry joined her on the deck.

Jerry inspected the tray with the half-eaten bowl of fruit. "Do you want anything else?"

"I'm fine. Thank you so much for the refreshments, and thank Gretchen again for me."

"I have a request." Cade jerked his thumb toward the beach. "Okay if we have a walk down to the beach?"

"You know as well as I do, it isn't private." Jerry unlatched the gate that led to a path to the sand.

"Yeah, but I also know we'll have to come back this way to get to our car, unless we walk around the rocks."

· "It's your house, Cade, or it will be in a few months." Jerry lifted his hand as they squeezed through the gate.

"I'm going to take off these boots." At the bottom of the steps, Lori sat down. "What did he mean the house was yours? Isn't it your parents'?"

"Actually, no. My parents signed the house over to me. It's mine." He scuffed the toe of his tennis shoe in the sand. "Let's go."

They slogged through the dry sand until they hit the shore. Lori's bare feet slapped along the wet sand, her shoulder bumping Cade's awkwardly until he put his arm around her and they moved as one.

"Why didn't you tell me you owned the house?"

He stopped and squinted at the horizon. "I don't know. It was in the works before I came out here. It was part of the reason for my visit. The place is already calling me back, and you just might be the siren's call I can't resist."

He turned her toward him and bent his head to touch his lips to hers. As his kiss brushed her mouth, her phone rang.

She pulled it out of her pocket. "It's Josh."

She cleared her throat. "Hey, Josh. What's up?"

"This is just some weird stuff, Lori."

Her heart jumped and she clutched the phone. "What? What happened?"

"You know Summer Larson's print was at Courtney's?"

"Yes?" A thrumming dread pounded against her eardrums and Cade was poking her and making hand gestures. "I'm putting this on Speaker for Summer's brother. Go on, Josh."

"We got a report of another missing woman. Roommate came home to an empty, disheveled house. A bloody print was found on the doorjamb, just like the other two scenes."

Cade grabbed her arm, and she answered Josh. "That's unusual, I guess. A coincidence."

"It's more than that, Lori. The bloody print belongs to Courtney Jessup."

Chapter Fourteen

When Lori ended the call, she sank to the sand and he dropped next to her. "What is going on, Lori?"

"I have no idea. What or who is tying these women together? Where are they? Are the prints part of some sick joke?" She gouged the sand with a stick. "Now I regret my suspension. I should've been the one to discover that."

"When can Josh confirm the name of the latest missing woman? You still have Summer's Brighter Days card with the names on it, right? You didn't give that one to Marino."

"I still have it. As soon as Josh contacts me with her name, I'll check it out. I'm also going to memorize those names for my stint at the center—in case I run across any of them."

"If we can get a picture of her, we can check the website again to see if she shows up like Courtney did, although there are more blurred faces than clear ones on the site."

Lori bunched her hands in the sand. "The one silver lining here is if the women's prints are at other crime scenes, it means they're not dead."

"I've been thinking ever since you mentioned Manson." Cade juggled a couple of broken shells from one hand to the other. "What if this situation is something like a cult? What if these women are involved in the kidnapping of other women?"

She cocked her head at him. "Do you think Summer would participate in something like that? She had her issues, but she was always so gentle and sweet, too sweet."

"Exactly—too sweet, easily manipulated. How do you think she got into the whole drug scene? It was because of some idiot boyfriend of hers. The guy left her with an addiction and a baby."

"A baby?" Lori's fingers curled into the wet sand, and a pulse throbbed against her temple. "Wh-what happened to the baby?"

"My mom made her get an abortion." The line of Cade's jaw hardened. "She never told anyone, not even the guy. He didn't deserve to know, anyway... loser."

Lori hopped to her feet and dusted the sand from her palms. "We should get going. I have a big day tomorrow. I still want to do some shopping for Loretta. I figure at a retreat like that, she might wear black leggings and rock and roll T-shirts."

"As long as I don't have to dress up like the anonymous money man again." He stood up next to her and brushed off the back of his jeans. "Why did you let it slip to Ella that I was going to be out of the country?"

"It was just a feeling. Courtney had no family here—no husband, no boyfriend. Summer was on her own." She touched his arm. "At least as far as Brighter Days knew. I thought I'd be a more appealing prospect for anything that might be going down there if I presented as adrift from my friends and family, too."

"That's interesting because I had the same feeling when I was there." He picked some debris from her hair and let it fly away in the wind. "That's why I turned away from you when you embarked on the tour, and didn't show an interest in your treatment. I hope we're both wrong."

"Why?"

"Because if Brighter Days prefers patients who are on their own, there is something nefarious going on there—and you're going to be right in the middle of it."

CADE DROPPED HER off at her house and returned to his hotel to squeeze in some work. He also planned to call Marino to see if he could find out anything about the search warrant at the treatment center.

Lori spent the rest of the day picking up some clothes for her stay at Brighter Days and some makeup to keep up her disguise while she was there.

The packet Ella had handed her indicated that she should bring clothes for the week, and that the support staff would be doing the laundry weekly. She didn't intend to be there for laundry day.

As she packed her bag, she replayed her conversation with Cade in her head. Would he really give up everything in New York to move back to LA? To her? The fact that the transfer of the Malibu house had occurred before he even came out here and before he ran into her made her feel a little better. At least he wouldn't be making the move solely for her. She'd be unable to stand that pressure—especially once he found out about the baby…and she'd have to tell him. But not tonight.

He was taking her out to dinner in Santa Monica for a last meal before her dive into Brighter Days Recovery. She wanted to meet Reed Dufrain. She hadn't asked Natasha about him because she didn't want to show any undue interest in or knowledge about the center. Just another lost girl looking for a place to land.

As she watered her plants—just in case she spent more than a few days at the rehab center—her phone rang and she crossed the room to pick it up. Her heart fluttered when she saw Cade's name. Not much had changed since high school.

"It's still a little early for dinner. What's up?"

"Get on your laptop and access the Brighter Days website." His voice had an edge to it, which caused her heart to flutter *and* flip-flop at the same time.

"Okay, what's the problem?" She spun her laptop around on the counter to face her and woke it up.

"You'll see in a minute. Should be obvious."

She brought up the Brighter Days website. "I'm here. Looks the same to me. I thought maybe they'd added my name and photo or something."

"It's not what they added. Go to the images and click through, like we did before."

She clicked the icon for the photos and scanned through them. Then she caught her breath. "There's no picture of Courtney."

"Exactly. Marino finally got back to me and said he hadn't needed to get a search warrant for the center because Reed Dufrain, himself, invited him back. I asked if they'd found anything connecting Summer and Courtney to the center, and he said they hadn't."

"The picture, I told Marino about the picture on the website. Did he show Natasha?"

"I asked him about that and he replied that he looked at the photos on the site and nobody looked like Courtney. I went back to the website and nobody looks like Courtney because they removed that picture."

Lori flattened a hand against her stomach. "That proves something suspicious is going on."

"Ah, you didn't screen capture that picture, did you?"

"I guess I don't know as much about computers as I thought I did. It didn't occur to me to do that. I suppose you didn't, either."

"Nope. You need to reconsider your stay, Lori."

"Don't be ridiculous. It's more important now

than ever. We know something's up with that place. Dufrain invited the cops in because they'd had time to sanitize everything."

"Then we have another item on the agenda at dinner tonight."

"Which is?"

"We have to establish a way that I can communicate with you while you're there. I need to know you're okay."

She tried to reassure him. "I even bought a burner phone to bring with me in case they let me keep it or want to search it, but my guess is they'll take it from me. In fact, I think that's in the pamphlet Ella gave me."

"You'd better not bring it at all. They'll wonder why you have a basic phone instead of one with all your contacts, apps and pictures on it."

"I can hide it."

"I don't think I wanna know where you plan to hide a phone."

"I have a compartment in my suitcase. They won't find it. It's not a maximum-security prison. Even inmates where Danny is smuggle in cell phones. They're not going to rip my bag apart."

"Hide it before I get there, and I'll see if I can find it. If I can, leave it. We'll think of something else."

By the time Cade picked her up, she'd finished packing, secured her phone in the lining of her bag and had her clothes laid out for tomorrow.

When he showed up on her doorstep, he made a

beeline for the suitcase. Crouching down, he tipped it on its side and unzipped it. He spent the next ten minutes mauling her carefully packed clothing.

Finally, he sat back on his heels. "You stumped me. I can't find it."

She practically skipped toward him and showed him the area behind the lining where the top and bottom of the suitcase met, creating a space. "It's in there. I'll be fine."

"Okay, that's step one. We're going to map out a meeting place or escape route for you."

"Escape route? Do you think it'll get to that point?"

"Both Summer and Courtney are connected to Brighter Days in some way, they're both gone, Trey was murdered when he was about to tell us something about the center and they scrubbed Courtney from their website. You need an escape route." He rubbed his hands together. "Are you up for burgers on the way?"

"Burgers on the way?" She assessed his faded jeans and dark T-shirt through narrowed eyes. "I thought you were dressed a little too casually for dinner out—even in Santa Monica."

"We need to find a way in and out of that place before I'm gonna let you walk into the lion's den."

She widened her eyes and blinked. "Tonight?"

"Yeah, burgers on the way?"

"Give me a minute to change. I'm not wearing my

good jeans, silk blouse and heels to crawl through the underbrush in Topanga Canyon."

FOR THE SECOND time that day, they wound their way up Topanga Canyon Boulevard, but this time they parked on a turn-off road near the entrance to the road that led to the Brighter Days Recovery Center. Cade had studied maps of the area while they ate their dinner in the car, and had discovered a hiking trail near the center.

He turned on the dome light and spread the map between them. Poking his finger in the middle of the forest, he said, "We should be able to see Brighter Days from this trail and figure out a path between the trail and the center—unless they encourage you to hike. Didn't we see hiking as an activity on the website?"

"We saw a lot of things on that website." Lori chewed on her lower lip. "I can join the hiking group, and we can figure out a way for me to get lost to meet up with you somewhere off the trail."

"Let's check it out." Cade refolded the map and they exited the car.

They walked up the road for several feet, Cade's backpack bouncing on his back, and ducked into an opening that started the trail called Skull Rock Loop.

Lori whispered, "I hope we don't find any actual skulls on the loop."

"I think it refers to the view you get of a rock

shaped like a skull. We're not going that far, so don't worry about it."

Cade had come prepared and whipped out a flashlight that he directed to the ground. "Watch this part. It drops down, but we should be okay in the dark. There are no cliffs or waterfalls."

"Or skulls." She traipsed down the trail, sticking close to Cade and his beam of light.

After hiking for about fifteen minutes, Cade grabbed her arm and pointed through the trees to their left. "There it is. Those are the lights of Brighter Days."

Lori ducked as if someone could look out those windows and see them. "What do you think? About a mile?"

"Not more than that." He canvassed the ground with his flashlight. "I don't see a branch-off path though. Maybe the residents of Brighter Days go up to the road to access this trail—like we did."

"They're so close out here, there has to be a way, even if it's not official."

Cade reached out to a bush and fingered the branches. "These are pushed back and broken."

They shimmied through the foliage, and although nobody had officially cleared the way, there was a definite path heading toward Brighter Days.

Cade said, "This is it. Single file, follow me."

They crunched and crackled down the path, sending a few night creatures skittering out of their way. When Cade stopped, Lori bumped into him, as she'd been so focused on her feet and not tripping over a root or stump.

He pulled her beside him and put his mouth to her ear. "We don't have to go any farther. Someone from Brighter Days must use this path. You took the tour. Can you tell where this ends at the center?"

"I think off the back lawn and patio, which run right up against the trees. It makes sense. Do a little yoga and stretching, maybe a little tai chi, and then hit the trail."

"You need to contact me tomorrow and let me know what's going on. If you're in trouble or you need to get away, we'll meet here." He jerked his thumb toward two trees, a dark hollow between them. "I'm going to tie some yarn on the branch, so you can find it. Duck between these two trees, and you'll have some cover. I'll meet you and I'll get you out of here."

Cade tied the yarn on the branch and they turned and hiked back to the road, keeping silent most of the way. When they got to the car, Lori said, "Seems a bit elaborate to me. They're not going to suspect anything about me. I'll do a little snooping, and they'll be none the wiser."

"I always feel better with a backup plan." He reversed out of the turnout, and they started the descent back to the coast. "Now, let's get you home for a good night's sleep."

She rubbed his thigh. "I had something else in

mind. You're not gonna leave a girl alone the night before she enters rehab, are you?"

"In that case…" He quirked his eyebrows up and down.

By the time they reached her house, she had Cade's backup plan memorized because he kept reciting it to her over and over. She had also memorized his cell phone number, so she could call him from the burner if she needed to.

Cade tossed his backpack in the corner of the room. "I'm going to drop you off at the Reel Inn, and you can take a car from there so it won't cost so much."

Lori sucked in her bottom lip. "If I take an app car, they're going to figure I have a phone with me."

"They're not going to know where your ride originated. You ordered a car from home and then left your phone there." He stepped toward her and squeezed her shoulders. "You don't have to do this."

"I have to do it more than ever now—Marino found nothing there and they scrubbed their website. We know something's up with that place." Hunching her shoulder, she twisted her head to the side and kissed his hand. "It'll be fine. I have my escape plan, and I know you have my back."

He reached around her and pulled her laptop toward the edge of the counter. "I was thinking— we should screenshot the rest of the photos on the Brighter Days website, just in case."

"Probably a good idea, or I can just take pics with my phone of each page."

He spun the laptop toward her so that she could enter her password. Then he accessed the website. He held out his hand. "You want me to do it?"

"I'll do it." She pulled out her phone, and as Cade clicked through each image, she snapped a photo with her phone.

"Can you send those to me? Looks like we can't have too many copies of this stuff."

"I will." She placed her phone facedown on the counter. "Let me wash my hands and face first."

She shrugged out of her hoodie on the way to the bathroom and splashed some water on her face, after washing the dirt and grime from the trail off her hands.

"Okay, I feel halfway human now." She traipsed back into the living room and stopped short.

Cade looked up from her phone in his hands, his head cocked to one side, a furrow between his eyebrows. "Whose baby is this?"

Lori swallowed the lump in her throat and curled her fingers around the hem of her T-shirt. "What baby?"

He waved the phone in the air and his voice rose. "There's a picture on your phone of you and a baby—a very small baby, looks newborn."

"Why are you looking at the pictures on my phone?" As soon as the words left her mouth, she knew it was the wrong thing to say.

Cade's blue eyes got a little wild, and his cheeks flushed. "I was sending myself the website photos. Why are you holding a baby in what looks like a hospital gown with a tube in your arm?"

She'd wanted to tell him, but not now, not this way.

Cade brought the phone to his face, his nose practically touching the screen. "Whose baby is this? Is this your baby?"

Lori expelled a long breath, her shoulders slumping with the effort. "It's ours."

Chapter Fifteen

The picture of a young, teary-eyed Lori cuddling a newborn baby with a thatch of brown hair on its head blurred before his eyes. The room tilted and Cade dropped down to the stool, the phone still clutched in his hand. "When? Where?"

Lori folded her hands in front of her, looking like the picture of innocence—but now he knew better. "We had a baby girl. I gave her up for adoption."

"We?" The word came out flat, barely above a whisper. Cade cleared his throat. "*We* had nothing to do with this because you neglected to tell me anything about it."

"How could I, Cade?" The folded hands knotted and she twisted her fingers. "Realistically, how could I have told you? You had your whole life mapped out in front of you—Harvard undergrad, Wharton business school. A teenage bride and a baby hardly fit that plan."

"Where did you get off making decisions about

my life for me? Those plans weren't even mine. Those were my father's dreams for me."

"But they became your dreams. You were looking for any excuse at the time to rebel against your dad. I would've handed you the perfect package. You would've jumped on it and then regretted me forever after."

"Package? Is that what a baby is?" He covered his face with his hands, so much of Lori's behavior that summer suddenly making sense. He should've known, should've seen something different. "Where is she?"

"She's with a good family in San Diego. Her parents are teachers, and she has a younger adopted brother."

"A-are you in touch with them?"

"No. It's a closed adoption until she's eighteen, when and if she chooses to track me…us down." She crossed her arms over her body in a protective move. "I pulled some strings to find out where she went, but I'd never disrupt her life. It was the right thing to do."

"And you made that determination all on your own."

"Of course, my parents advised me. They helped me. Sent me to an aunt in San Diego to have the baby. I came back here after I gave birth and started the winter quarter at UCLA."

Dragging a hand through his hair, he said, "Your mother counseled you not to tell me?"

She dropped her lashes over her eyes. "She wanted me to tell you."

"You didn't take her advice about that." He smacked the counter with the flat of his hand and relished the sting that traveled up his arm. "Were you ever going to tell me?"

"Believe it or not, I was planning to tell you before you went back to New York. I realized…" She lifted her shoulders.

"You realized you'd kept something from me that I had every right to know about." He jumped from the stool, knocking it to the ground. "You lied to me back then. You've been lying to me on this trip."

"I was trying to protect you. I didn't want to ruin your life." She shoved her hands in her pockets, looking small and vulnerable, and another wave of sorrow crashed over him when he thought about her on her own in San Diego, pregnant, delaying college, giving birth without him by her side, having someone take that sad photo of her and the baby she'd have to give up.

"That was up to me, Lori. Who says you didn't ruin my life by not telling me about my daughter?" He hooked his hand around the back of the stool and righted it.

He wanted to ask her a million questions about their daughter, but he could barely look at her.

Instead, he swooped down to snag his backpack. "Look, I gotta go."

"What about tomorrow?"

"I'll pick you up at noon, just like we discussed." He stepped outside and clicked the door softly behind him. Closing his eyes, he took a deep breath of the salty air.

By the time he got back to his hotel, the shock had subsided, leaving him with a dull ache in the pit of his stomach. How could Lori justify what she'd done?

He stripped off his clothes and showered, scrubbing his skin so hard it stung. He didn't know what he was trying to wash away—the memories of that time, how he'd shrugged off Lori's changed behavior, how he'd embraced his father's plans for him, or Lori's deception.

As he climbed into bed, his cell phone on the nightstand pinged. He reached for it and opened the text from Lori. She'd texted him the picture of her and their baby girl.

He fell asleep clutching the phone to his heart.

THE NEXT DAY, Lori wiped her damp palms against the thighs of her black jeans before opening the front door to Cade. Sleep had escaped her the night before, but at least the dark circles beneath her eyes matched her persona of the struggling addict.

She stepped outside, dragging her suitcase behind her, and mumbled a barely-there greeting.

Reaching past her for the handle of her bag, he said, "I'll get this."

She followed his stiff back out to his car, resisting the urge to throw herself at him and apologize profusely. Reviewing the dramatic scene in her head last night, she realized she'd never told him she was sorry for withholding the truth from him. Was it too late now?

As she slid into the passenger seat, he hauled the suitcase into the trunk of his rental. He sat behind the wheel, and she spun toward him. "I'm sorry, Cade. I'm sorry I didn't tell you about my pregnancy or tell you about the baby later. I was scared, stupid and had too much pride to use a pregnancy to snag you. Your parents would've hated me—even more than they already did, and half of my family would've disowned me for getting pregnant before marriage. It seemed like the best plan at the time."

He held up his hand to stop the flow of words. "I understand why you didn't tell me."

She studied his white knuckles on the wheel of the car. Was that an acceptance of her apology? Not quite. "D-did you get the photo I sent you?"

"I did, thanks. Do you have any more?"

"No." She clasped her hands between her knees, accepting the needling pain at the old wound as payment for her deceit. "Although I have a general idea where she lives, I wanted to honor her privacy and her parents' wishes. I've never looked her up or even tried to catch a glimpse of her at play or school."

"She'd be…"

"Nine. She's nine years old now." Lori held her breath waiting for other questions, questions she knew he must have.

"She's healthy?" He relaxed his grip on the wheel and started driving.

"She was a healthy, full-term baby and weighed seven pounds, eight ounces at birth. Sh-she was beautiful." Her nose stung and she blinked her eyes, as she turned her head and stared at the traffic.

"Was your mother with you?"

"She was there. It killed her almost as much as it did me when we left the hospital without the baby. I met her parents, and they were wonderful. I'm sure she has a great life."

Cade let out a long ragged breath. "It must've been hard on you. That's what cuts me the most—the thought of you in San Diego, going through this pregnancy on your own while I was at college going to frat parties and football games."

"It wasn't easy." She sniffed and squared her shoulders. "But soon enough, I was at college going to frat parties and basketball games—secure in the knowledge that I'd done the right thing for our baby, that she'd have two mature parents who wanted to raise her with no regrets. She deserved that."

"Are you going to make contact with her when she turns eighteen?"

"I'm going to leave it up to her. Her parents may have already told her by now that they adopted her. If she's interested in finding me, I'm open to that discovery. I'm open to a relationship, if she wants that. I'm also okay if she doesn't." She traced a pattern on the window. "What do you think you would've done if I'd told you back then?"

Cade accelerated onto the freeway with a burst of speed. "I would've married you."

Lori didn't have much to say after that proclamation, and Cade had retreated into a morose silence, not even emerging to go over her escape plan from Brighter Days, if that became necessary. At this point, he probably didn't care if she stayed at Brighter Days forever.

Finally, he pulled onto the street beside the Reel Inn and parked the car. "It's probably not a good idea for me to come inside with you. Order your car from your regular phone now, and then leave it with me. Don't worry. I won't do any more snooping. I don't even know your password. I saw the photo of the baby because I picked up the phone as soon as you put it down—just to send the Brighter Days pictures to myself."

"You don't have to explain yourself. I know you weren't going through my phone." She slid her cell out of her purse and pulled up the car app. "You don't have to be on call for me. Nothing is going to happen. I'll have a look around and decide the place isn't for me after a few days."

"Don't be obstinate. You don't always know what's best, and I'd appreciate it if you'd stop trying to control my actions."

"Whatever." She lifted her eyebrows and blew out a breath, as she scheduled a pickup in forty-five minutes. "I'm going to eat some lunch first. I'll try to contact you tonight. Keep on Marino…if you want."

"I plan to." He popped the trunk and exited the car.

Sighing, she dropped her phone in the cup holder and joined him, her boots crunching the gravel beneath them. "Thanks for helping out with all this. I'm hopeful I'll find something."

He landed a hard kiss on her mouth. "Just be careful."

She wheeled her suitcase up to the door of the restaurant and watched Cade drive off with tears in her eyes. She'd really messed up, but she felt stronger about the decision she'd made nine years ago than ever before.

If she'd told Cade about the pregnancy, he would've done the honorable thing and married her. His parents probably would have cut him off. Neither of them could've afforded college right away. He would've resented her for his missed opportunities. She would've resented him for resenting her, and they would've taken it out on each other and ended up getting divorced.

He couldn't see that now through the haze of hurt, but maybe one day he'd come around—maybe not soon enough to repair their relationship on this visit and maybe they'd never have another chance.

Right now, she had to focus on playing this role to help his sister, Courtney and the other nameless woman who'd gone missing. Josh hadn't gotten back to her yet with an identity for the third victim but as the police had found Courtney's prints at this woman's place, the connection between the three of them was undeniable.

Lori ordered a bowl of clam chowder and toyed with it as she waited for her ride. When she saw her car arrive outside, she left a half-full bowl of soup and dragged her suitcase outside.

The driver helped her load it into the trunk, and they took off on the now familiar drive to Brighter Days. She had to direct the driver down the final road, as his GPS was giving him confusing signals to the bucolic center tucked away in the canyon.

He pulled around to the side where she and Cade had parked before. As she wheeled her suitcase toward the side door, it opened, and a thin man of medium height with close-cropped hair and a full beard stepped onto the stone walkway.

Lori recognized him from the website as Reed Dufrain, and her heart skipped a beat. He didn't offer to help her, nor did he talk or greet her in any way. He watched.

She swallowed as she approached him, her eyes behind her sunglasses studying the still face before her. He didn't move one muscle, but his light-colored eyes seemed to probe her very soul as she approached. She'd have to be careful with this one.

She clattered to a stop before him, and stuck out her hand. "I'm Loretta Garcia. I'm checking in today."

"I'm Reed Dufrain, the center's director." He had some kind of accent she couldn't readily identify, and she jumped when he suddenly snapped his fingers, ignoring her outstretched hand.

As if hovering nearby awaiting his command, a young man, dressed all in white, appeared next to Dufrain and smiled at Lori, his teeth bright against his brown skin. "I'm Peron. I'll take your bag and show you to your room."

She dropped her hand awkwardly and handed off her bag to Peron. She shoved her sunglasses to the top of her head as she walked past Dufrain, meeting his eyes directly for the first time. An instant chill dripped down her spine.

The man had no lashes or very light lashes that seemed at odds with his brown beard. Coupled with his light blue eyes, it gave him an otherworldly quality. He probably played that up to the patients to make them think he was on some different plane.

Dufrain turned to cup her elbow in his hand, a scent of sandalwood wafting over her. "I'll accompany you to your room, Loretta, and we'll discuss your program. You're off all substances now?"

"That's right. I quit cold turkey with some help from Narcotics Anonymous, but my main support person is out of town right now for an extended period and I feel shaky."

"Understandable." His fingers pinched her flesh through her jacket, as if he feared she'd take flight at any moment.

Should she?

She cleared her throat. "Where's Natasha?"

"She's busy in the office. You won't see much of her during your stay, as she handles the business end of the center and isn't involved in the treatment programs."

As the heels of her boots clattered on the wooden floors, she realized Dufrain was barefoot beneath his wide-legged trousers. His footsteps whispered next to hers, and he moved as silently and gracefully as a cat.

He glided down a hallway of closed doors, propelling her along until he threw open a door to the right. Light flooded a sparsely but beautifully furnished room. "This is yours. It's quiet right now because most of the guests are at an after-lunch yoga and meditation session. You still have time to join, if you'd like."

"I'd very much like that. Where should I go once I change?"

Dufrain flicked his fingers in the air, toward a button on the wall beside the door. "You can summon Peron or one of our other attendants to show you the way when you're ready. I'll leave a copy of your schedule on your bed and you can peruse that at your leisure and let me know if you have any questions."

Lori pointed to the call button. "Do I contact you the same way?"

"That's for the attendants…or in an emergency, but the attendants can always reach me."

"Emergency?" She tilted her head.

"Our guests are in different stages of recovery, Loretta. I'm sure you recall the discomfort of detoxing."

"Oh, I do. Nice to know Brighter Days is equipped to handle anything."

Dufrain put his hands together as if in prayer and dipped his head. "I'll leave you to change now. I hope you find everything you're looking for here."

So did she.

Dufrain stopped at the door. "Who did you say referred you to us?"

She crouched beside her suitcase where Peron had left it on the floor and unzipped it. Without looking up, she said, "A friend who wishes to remain anonymous. It obviously worked for her, or she wouldn't have referred me."

The soft click of the door was the only signal that he'd left. Lori fell back on her heels and huffed out a breath. The man put her on edge. It must just be because she was here under false pretenses, and he seemed so…all knowing.

She dug through her clothes for a pair of black yoga pants and a long T-shirt. As she tugged off her jeans, she leaned over the bed to read the schedule Dufrain had left there.

She could choose from several activities each hour, but the center expected you to choose something. You couldn't sit around in your room all day—

unless you were ill—and he had a few nurses on staff.

She'd do this yoga, get the lay of the land, do a survey of some of the other patients—guests, he'd called them—and do a little snooping around when she could.

Forty-five minutes later, stretched out and refreshed, Lori lounged by the pool with several other women who'd been doing yoga with her. They had a free hour or so before the next set of activities started, so a few of them dangled their feet in the water while others reclined on the lounges with their eyes closed. She wasn't going to get anything out of them, so she turned to the woman sitting next to her at the pool, a tall, thin blonde with alabaster skin.

"I'm Loretta. I just arrived."

"I figured that since I haven't seen you here before. I'm Lucy." The woman lifted her hand where she'd been trailing it in the water and offered it to Lori.

Lori clicked through the names in her head from the Brighter Days business card, but Lucy wasn't one of them. Strike one. Lori shook her hand, water and all. "Nice to meet you, Lucy. How long have you been here?"

"Too long." She wrinkled her slightly turned-up nose. "My husband made me come here, and is making me stay for the full month as a condition to continue our marriage. We have a little girl."

"That's nice." Cupping some water in her hand

and dumping it on the pool deck, Lori asked, "Is it working for you?"

"I'm clean and sober." Lucy held up her hand as if to testify. "I suppose it works—at least here. Hope it holds for the real world, or I might lose my girl."

"And Reed Dufrain?" Lori twisted her head over her shoulder, pretending to investigate a sound by the door, but really making sure Dufrain wasn't tiptoeing around the pool. "Is he as good as they say?"

Lucy flattened her hands on her thighs. "His program is effective, but he does have his favorites."

"He has favorites?" Lori's pulse quickened.

Lucy lifted her sunglasses and studied Lori with her green eyes. "Don't hold your breath. You're not gonna be one of his faves."

"Not that I want to be, but why do you say that?"

"You're not messed up enough. Dufrain seems to gravitate toward the worst cases. He isolates them from the rest of us once he makes his picks. I've seen it happen a couple times since I've been here." Lucy lifted her shoulders. "Maybe he just figures they need more help than the rest of us. The yoga, meditation, cooking sessions, hikes—those seem to work for those of us who are already off the substances."

Lori turned her head to survey the women stretched out on chaise lounges under umbrellas and whispered, "Any of those his favorites?"

Dismissing them with a wave of her hand, Lucy said, "His pets wouldn't be out here. They mostly stay cooped up in their rooms and have private sessions with Reed. They're probably doing some other kind of intensive treatment program. Hey, let's be happy we're not in that boat."

"Amen to that."

She continued chatting with Lucy about their own particular vices and Lucy's daughter, until it was time to select the next activity. Lucy was participating in the group therapy session, so Lori decided to follow her there.

Had Summer been one of Dufrain's favorites? Why did she have his card in a safe deposit box? Had she been messed up when she'd arrived here?

After the group session, she walked with Lucy back to their rooms. When they were clear of the other women, Lori asked, "Did you know someone named Summer here, or Courtney? It would've been earlier in your stay."

Lucy twisted up her mouth to one side. "Don't think so."

They turned a corner in the hallway and Lucy jerked her thumb to the side, indicating a smaller hallway off the main one. She lowered her voice. "You asked about the pets? They usually bunk down there. Reed spends a lot of his time in this area."

Nodding, Lori said, "They must need that extra help."

The guests were supposed to use this time to shower and change from their daytime activities to meet in the kitchen for some cooking lessons on preparing healthy food. With everyone in their rooms, this might give Lori an opportunity to check out Dufrain's favorite guests. She already knew the doors wouldn't be locked, as locks weren't allowed.

When Lucy turned into her own room, Lori sailed into hers and made a quick change of clothes. Then she poked her head out her door and looked both ways down the hallway.

On bare feet as quiet as Dufrain himself, Lori crept back to the smaller hallway, where two doors faced each other. She tried the first door, easing it open onto a clearly empty room. She padded to the next door and inched it open, peeking inside.

A dark-haired woman lay prone on the bed in the darkened room, her eyes half-closed. Lori glanced over her shoulder quickly before slipping inside the room and softly closing the door behind her.

She tiptoed to the bedside and crouched beside the woman. "Hello? Are you all right?"

The woman's slack mouth moved slightly, and Lori bent her head closer to her lips and repeated. "Are you all right? Should I call someone?"

The woman's hand curled around Lori's wrist in a tight grip that startled her, and she jerked back. Rasping words came from the woman's mouth, and Lori leaned in again. "What did you say?"

The woman licked her cracked lips and widened her dilated eyes. "Not Reed. Please don't call Reed."

Chapter Sixteen

With her heart pounding, Lori dropped to her knees. Wasn't this woman supposed to be one of Reed's favorites? "Why not? Why not call Reed?"

Lori heard a bump outside the door followed by Reed Dufrain's voice, and her gaze darted wildly around the Spartan room for a place to hide. The doorknob turned as he continued to talk, and Lori collapsed to the floor and scooted beneath the bed. She twitched the bed skirt into place seconds before she heard Dufrain's footsteps in the room.

He snapped the door behind him, and Lori released a tiny breath from her nose, stirring a fine film of dust on the floor. If she sneezed now, it would be all over.

In the small space that existed between the hem of the bed skirt and the hardwood floor, Lori spied Dufrain's bare toes as he stood next to the bed. The blood roared in her ears so loudly, she could barely hear his words.

"How are you today, Karenna? I think you should

be up and about soon, and then you'll get to leave. You'll like that, won't you?"

Karenna made a gurgling noise, and Lori squeezed her eyes closed. Karenna, Karenna. That was one of the names on Summer's card. This couldn't be a coincidence.

She hoped Karenna didn't think Lori had summoned Dufrain to her bedside. She was obviously terrified of him…and Lori should be, too.

"Just a few more…" something clinked on a metal tray as Dufrain paused "…shots of this and you won't be able to live without it."

Lori clenched her jaw. Wasn't he supposed to be curing addictions instead of introducing them? What was he doing to Karenna?

Karenna thrashed in the bed, shifting the covers, creating a bigger space between the bed skirt and the floor. Lori noticed a strand of her black wig very close to Dufrain's foot, but she feared the slightest movement would alert Dufrain to her presence.

"Not to worry." Skin slapped against skin, and Lori curled her nails into the hard wood. "I have enough of this magic potion to keep you well supplied and feeling good for as long as I need you. I'll lessen the dose today, and you'll be walking and talking within days. But make no mistake about it, Karenna, you'll need it and only I can give it to you."

Karenna made a muffled cry, and Lori smashed her nose into the floor to keep quiet.

Dufrain spent several seconds more hovering over

Karenna on the bed before his footsteps whispered across the room, and then the door snapped shut.

Lori lay still for another minute and then shimmied out from beneath the bed. She loomed over Karenna, but the drug had sedated the woman again. She lifted Karenna's limp arm, squinting at the needle tracks on the inside of her elbow, some old and one very fresh. Her stomach turned. Dufrain had shot her up with something.

She slipped out of the room and scurried back to her own. When she closed the door behind her, she fell across her bed. Dufrain was some kind of monster. He was taking vulnerable women, and under the pretense of helping them overcome one addiction, he was addicting them to something else. What was it? Heroin? Some kind of opioid?

She and Cade had left the powder they'd found at Summer's place in that shoebox. Now she wanted to get her hands on it and have it tested. Was that what Dufrain had injected into Karenna? Had Summer and Courtney been addicted to the same substance?

She needed to reach Cade tonight and tell him to get that drug from Summer's. She had a friend who could test it for her—no questions asked.

What had she stumbled onto? Whatever it was, she knew it was serious enough to get her killed.

LATER THAT NIGHT after a healthy dinner of brown rice, stir-fried vegetables and soy curls, Lori crouched before her suitcase and unzipped the compartment where she'd stashed her burner phone.

Peron had dumped out her purse to search it and then did a cursory search of her suitcase. He'd never thought to unzip the lining of the bag.

Lori rolled the phone into a towel and padded to the patio in the back to join some of the other women in the hot tub. They obviously had no idea what was going on in those other rooms. Did Dufrain have someone in addition to Karenna captive in that hallway? Were Diana and Chelsea, the other names on the card, here, too?

She shoved her towel next to a bush and slid into the hot bubbly water next to Shannon, her cooking buddy.

Shannon handed her a flute with fizzing golden liquid. "Don't get too excited. It's sparkling apple cider, not champagne."

"I'll take it, thanks." Lori sipped the chilled, tart liquid and maneuvered until a jet of bubbles hit her lower back. "That feels good."

One of the other women, Jessica, submerged her shoulders beneath the water until just her head bobbed on the surface. "Yeah, this place would be great if they added weed and wine to the nightly activities."

A few of the women laughed, but some didn't appreciate her humor and a couple of them used the opportunity to get out.

"Bye-bye." Jessica waved at their backs. "How

do they think they're going to cope in the real world when someone does more than just talk about it?"

Lori cupped some water in her hand and sprinkled it on the deck. "It's not easy."

"Oh, right. You were clean when you came in here." Jessica wrapped one of her dark curls around her finger. "If I was able to get clean on my own without rehab, I'd stay far, far away from places like this. Despite its obvious comforts, it's still a prison. What made you come here?"

A prison? Karenna would have to agree.

Lori draped her arms across the edge of the hot tub and lightly paddled her feet. "I had a friend helping me out, and he had to leave for work out of the country. I'm still wavering on the edge, and didn't think I could make it without his support. So far, so good, but I didn't realize the center took people in the throes of their addiction…like Karenna."

The other women met her words with dead silence. She studied their faces. "What? What did I say wrong?"

"Nothing." Shannon took a swig of apple juice as if it were booze. "It's just that we don't talk about guests like Karenna…or Diana."

Lori gulped. Another name from the card. She asked, "Diana?"

"She's like Karenna—on the Cocaine Corridor or Heroin Hallway, if you prefer." Jessica gave a short hiccup of a laugh.

Lori looked from Shannon to Jessica. "What does that mean? They're still addicted?"

"Aren't we all?" Shannon smoothed her hands over the surface of the choppy water.

"The thing with those women…" Jessica leaned forward, her chin skimming the water "…they came in like the rest of us—some still high as kites, some one day clean and a few like you, but the difference between us and them is that we're all taking the steps to get better and those two don't seem to be getting any better. Reed doesn't like it when we talk about them."

Shannon said, "He doesn't want us to dwell on the negative."

Jessica snorted. "He doesn't want us to dwell on his failures."

Lori swirled the remainder of her apple juice in her glass, where it caught the lights around the pool and sparkled. Was that the story Reed spread? The women had relapsed or couldn't get with the program? He had to isolate them and offer special treatment?

She asked, "Why doesn't he just discharge them?"

"He wants to help everyone." Shannon scrunched her eyebrows over her nose. "He doesn't want to give up on anyone."

He wants to take advantage of them.

Jessica seemed all talked out, and as she placed her glass on the tray, she said, "I'm going to bed, ladies. If you see a hot guy wandering around, send him my way."

Shannon winked at Lori. "There's always Peron."

"A hot, *straight* guy." Jessica rose from the water and it sluiced from her body in steaming rivulets. "You two coming? Curfew in less than thirty."

"I am." Shannon stood up to join her, the water lapping around her knees. "Loretta?"

"I'm going to spend a few more minutes in here." She placed her glass on the tray and tipped in a little more juice. "Don't worry about the tray. I'll take it in."

The tray would also give her an excuse for being outside on her own. She said good-night to the other women and sipped her juice for a few minutes. When she spied more lights in the main building going out, she staggered from the hot tub and grabbed her towel.

She jogged across the sprawling lawn toward the tree line. The entrance to the path that met up with the Skull Rock Loop nestled just beyond those trees. If she had any sense at all, she'd make a beeline for that trail and never look back.

She could call Marino and let him make sense of this, but then she'd have to explain how she knew all about Karenna and Diana.

Instead, she reached for the phone buried in the towel and ducked between some bushes, twigs stabbing the bottoms of her feet. She punched in Cade's phone number, and he didn't even wait for the first ring to end.

"Hello?" Cade's voice sounded businesslike. He must still be fuming about her pregnancy.

"That's it? Hello? Who did you expect from this number?"

He let out a breath across the line. "Just in case it wasn't you, I didn't want to use your name."

"You're really getting into this."

He cut her off. "Stop, Lori. Are you all right? Are you ready to leave?"

"I found something out today, Cade, and it's bad."

"Summer. Did you find out what happened to Summer?"

"Not yet, but Reed Dufrain is a messed-up guy. He's evil. He's singling out a few of the women who come through these doors, and he's…he's making them worse."

"What does that mean?"

She didn't intend to tell Cade about her close call with Dufrain in Karenna's room. She didn't want to freak him out any more than he already was.

"He's drugging some of these women, addicting them to some substance. I have no idea why, and I don't know what he's using." She glanced over her shoulder. "There's something else."

"What?"

"The two women he's targeting for special treatment are Karenna and Diana—two of the names from the card."

Cade whistled through his teeth. "I've got more bad news for you. The third missing woman, where Courtney's prints were found? Her name is Chelsea Kim. We've identified all three names on that card, and they're all in trouble."

"Karenna and Diana are here, but where are Summer, Courtney and Chelsea?"

Cade swore. "Lori, get out of there, and we'll call the police. We'll tell Marino."

She hissed over the phone. "Are you kidding? I have no proof. Dufrain will clean things up again before Marino comes out here. Just give me another day or two to figure this out."

"Does anyone suspect you of anything?"

"No. The other clients here know about those women Dufrain is dosing, but they just think they relapsed and Dufrain is treating them." She growled into the phone. "He's treating them, all right."

"I don't like this, Lori. The man is dangerous."

"I've got something to keep you busy and your mind off...everything." She sucked in her bottom lip. "You need to get those drugs from Summer's closet and deliver them to a guy I know. I want to find out what she has."

"A guy? The police?"

"Yeah, he is a cop, but he'll do this off the record if I ask him. If you ask him."

"Great, I'll be running around LA with illegal drugs in my possession, meeting a dirty cop."

"He's not dirty. He worked undercover vice for

years and he knows people, discreet people. You don't want the cops knowing Summer had those drugs, do you?"

"Okay, give me his name and number."

"His name is Trevor Jansen. I don't have his number on me, but you can get it from my cell phone. My passcode is the year of my birth. Just mention my name, tell him as little as you like—oh, hell, you know what to do."

"Be careful, for God's sake. And Lori?"

"Yeah?"

"Just so you know, I hired a private investigator to find our daughter."

Lori's knees wobbled and she almost sank to the ground. "Don't do this, Cade."

"Don't worry. I'm not going to interfere in her life. I just want to know more about her parents, her family. Give me that, will you?"

She knew Cade had to wrest back some kind of control over this situation. "I understand, as long as you don't contact her. We have to think of her first. And no sending her anonymous donations of money, or anything."

"I'm not going to do anything like that."

She loosened her grip on the phone. "Okay, thanks for giving me a heads-up."

"You'd better get back before you're missed. I'll retrieve the drugs from Summer's and contact this guy, Trevor. Stay out of trouble. Don't draw attention to yourself…and don't take any strange vitamins."

As soon as Lori ended the call, she deleted it from the phone and rolled the burner back up in her towel. She ducked out of the underbrush and squelched across the damp lawn. When she reached the deck, she almost slipped, as a dark figure rose from a lounge chair.

Peron had changed from his all-white ensemble to an all-black one. "Loretta, right?"

"Th-that's right." She put a hand to her throat. "You scared me."

His mouth widened into a smile. "I can say the same thing. I thought that maybe a mountain lion had crossed onto the grounds. It's happened before."

"Oh, no. If I had known that, I wouldn't have gone over to the bushes to investigate the noise I heard." She swept an arm toward the tray of empty glasses on one of the tables. "I came back to get the tray, heard a noise and skipped over there to investigate. I hope it wasn't a mountain lion."

"Maybe you scared him." Peron tapped his wrist. "It's past curfew."

"Is it?" She sidled to the table and lifted the tray. "Didn't realize it was so late."

"I'll take that. We wouldn't want Reed to catch you out after curfew."

"Why? What's the punishment for that? Extra yoga sessions or an extra helping of soy curls?" She forced a laugh that sounded hollow.

The whites of Peron's eyes shone in the darkness, and he put a finger to his lips. "I won't tell on you."

With her mouth dry, Lori spun away from him and strode toward the building. "Good night."

She hurried along the corridor and slipped into her room. Gripping the handle behind her, she pressed her back against the door, her heart racing. She couldn't tell if Peron believed her or not, or if he'd tell Reed about her nocturnal sojourn, despite his assurance.

Then her gaze stumbled across her suitcase in the corner, and she froze. Someone had been in her room tonight and had moved her bag. Whether Peron told Reed about finding her out after curfew or not didn't seem to matter anymore.

Somehow, someway, she'd gotten onto Reed Dufrain's radar—and that was a very bad development.

Chapter Seventeen

Cade sat under the umbrella at the hot dog stand with a bag of drugs in his pocket and a sheen of sweat on his forehead. Only Lori could get him into a situation like this. Although to be fair to her, he put the blame for this squarely on Summer.

A motorcycle roared up to the curb, and a lean, dark man hopped off, pulling a helmet from his head. Trevor said he'd be arriving on a bike, and he even sort of looked like a cop despite the black jeans and motorcycle boots. He'd told Cade he didn't work undercover anymore.

He stopped at the table and put his helmet on the attached seat. "I'm gonna grab a dog. You want something?"

Cade raised his soda. "I'm good."

Several minutes later, Trevor returned with a hot dog, dripping chili, in one hand and a drink in the other. He stepped over the bench with a long stride and sat straddling the bench, facing Cade. "Where's Lori? I heard she was suspended from the job."

"She was. She's taking some time away."

Trevor shook his head as he bit into the hot dog. He wiped his mouth with a napkin and crumpled it in his fist. "She's good at her job, but sometimes she rubs people the wrong way because she's a little too overzealous. You know what I mean?"

Trevor had no idea how overzealous Lori had gotten. "She always feels like she has to right an injustice. You know about her brother."

"I do." Trevor licked some chili from his fingers and grabbed another napkin. "Between you and me, Danny Del Valle is guilty as hell, unidentified print or not."

"I think so, too, but…" Cade ran a finger along the seam of his lips "…I don't tell her that."

"I tried that once, and she nearly bit my head off. I guess it's hard to face the fact that your brother is a killer."

Cade toyed with the plastic bag of drugs in his jacket pocket and said, "You always want to believe the best about the people you love."

"I get that, but Danny's arrest and conviction have colored Lori's life. Like you said—she hates to see an injustice, and it drives her to do stupid things sometimes."

Cade figured he'd better break off the direction of this conversation before he presented Trevor with the drugs and Lori's new scheme.

Lifting his shoulders, he said, "We all have our weaknesses."

"That's for sure." Trevor washed down another bite of his hot dog with a sip from his cup. "What can I do for you…or Lori?"

"It's really a favor to me. Lori just said you might be able to help without forcing me to go through regular channels."

"Happy to help. I owe Lori. My girlfriend's a PI, and Lori has come through for her a few times running prints for her." Trevor wedged his hands on his knees. "Whaddya got?"

Cade pinched the plastic baggie of drugs between his fingers and drew it out of his pocket. "My sister is missing, and I found this white powder hidden away in her closet. She's had substance abuse problems in the past, so this isn't a surprise to me, but Lori couldn't tell me what type of drug this was. She said you had some connections."

Trevor held out his hand and Cade dropped the packet in his palm. He whistled through his teeth. "This looks like some of that wicked China Girl we've been seeing on the street. You see the pink tint? Highly addictive, less deadly than some of the other strains."

"China Girl?"

"One of the many street names for fentanyl." He jiggled the baggie. "This is a new product that's hit the street just in the past year. We don't know where it's coming from yet. You said your sister had it?"

"Yeah, and she's missing."

"Is your sister a dealer?"

"What?" Cade wiped a hand across his mouth. "No. She doesn't need money. There wouldn't be any reason for her to be selling drugs."

"Unless she's addicted and is getting her fix as a reward for selling." Trevor waved the packet in the air, and Cade looked around.

Good thing he was with a cop.

"This looks like it's packaged to sell. It's about the right amount, and it has a number stamped in the corner of the baggie, as if it's one of many."

Knots twisted in Cade's gut. Was this what Summer had been doing? Was that why she was missing now?

"Can you tell for sure? Lori said you had a way to test it."

"I can't, but I know someone who can." Trevor pocketed the plastic bag, and Cade relaxed his muscles for the first time since retrieving the drugs from Summer's house.

Trevor picked up the last bite of his dog. "Can I ask why you're not going to the police with this?"

"My sister's missing, she's an addict and I found drugs at her house." Cade spread his hands. "Why do you think?"

"You got a point." Trevor popped the hot dog in his mouth. "I'll take care of this, and I'll contact Lori when I have some info. If your sister has any shady acquaintances, I'd appreciate a name. We know this pink China Girl is coming from a particular source, and we want to nail it down."

Cade didn't want to mention Reed Dufrain until Lori had left Brighter Days. If he thought she'd ID'd him and she was still under his control there, there was no telling what he might do. He obviously had henchmen on the outside. There's no way he slashed Lori's tires or killed Trey himself.

Trevor cleared his throat. "You got a name?"

"Can't think of anyone." Cade shook his head.

"I'll get this done." Trevor smacked the table as he got up, and a minute later, he zoomed off on his bike.

Cade rattled the ice in his empty drink, and then lobbed it into the nearby trash can. If Reed Dufrain had facilitated Summer's addiction to this China Girl stuff during her stay at Brighter Days and Summer was selling it for him to maintain her supply, that meant Lori was in grave danger at that place.

And he was going to get her out of there.

THE DAY AFTER her run-in with Peron, Lori kept her head down and participated in as many activities as she could squeeze into her day. She didn't want to stand out to Reed or anyone else. She didn't even know if she could trust those women in the hot tub last night. Jessica had seemed too chatty for her own good, and Shannon had seemed pretty dedicated to Reed. What if one of them was a plant to draw out the new girl?

She avoided both Jessica and Shannon…and Peron. She'd seen him once today, and he'd given her that slightly sinister grin that she didn't like one bit.

She wanted to get back into Karenna's room to make sure the woman was okay, but if anyone caught her there, she'd have a hard time dancing her way out of it.

She'd seen Reed around a few times, floating through the compound in his baggy cotton pants and tunic, but he'd barely given her a nod. Maybe the staff routinely searched all the rooms at night for any contraband. She'd signed off on staying in a facility that didn't lock the rooms, so she couldn't complain now.

Peron knew animals haunted the wilderness around them, so her story had probably made sense to him. She was fitting in just like any other guest. Maybe her paranoia wasn't as justified as she imagined.

Her next goal was to snag a sample of whatever Reed was giving Karenna. If she had something solid to take to Marino, he could make a move. Of course, she'd have to explain her presence at Brighter Days and she couldn't admit to an addiction, not in her line of work.

Lori gritted her teeth through the last activity of the day—art therapy—and then returned to her room during the quiet time. She knew she had several minutes to visit Karenna before Reed showed up with her potion, and this time she took her burner phone with her. It might be basic, but it still had a camera.

Wearing her paint-spattered smock from earlier, she crept down the hallway to Karenna's room. She pressed her ear to the door with her fingers around the handle. She turned the handle and bumped the door with her hip.

Unlike her own airy room, all the shades in this room were pulled down and the room itself faced north. Through the dim light from a few slats in the blinds, Lori could make out Karenna's form on top of the bed.

She tiptoed toward her and crouched beside the bed.

"Karenna?"

Karenna's dark lashes fluttered and she held up her hands as if to ward off an attack.

Lori put her finger to her lips. "I'm not going to hurt you. Why is Reed doing this? Do you know what he wants?"

Karenna worked her mouth and a line of drool dribbled from the corner.

Lori plucked a tissue from the box on the nightstand and dabbed at the moisture. "I'm here to help you, but I need to know what's going on. Why is Reed drugging you?"

Karenna tried again, firming her lips into a line. "Drugs."

"I know he has you on drugs, but why?"

"Control." The word proved too much for Karenna, and she closed her eyes.

"Why does he want to control you, Karenna? What does he want you to do? Where are the others?"

Karenna's lids flew open. "Below. Go."

"Below where?"

"Go." Karenna's eyes darted to the door.

She obviously knew Reed's schedule, too.

Lori patted Karenna's dry hand. "I'll be back. Don't worry. The police are going to put a stop to this."

She crept back to the door and cracked it open. Her gaze shifted back and forth and she slipped into the hallway. As she made her way to the main corridor, she heard Reed's voice and the trundling wheels of a cart.

She'd left it too long. She spun around and tried the door to the empty room, but someone had locked it—not all the rooms were on the honor system.

As the voices and wheels grew louder, Lori raced down the hallway to the door at the end. She shoved the metal bar to exit and stumbled outside, facing a bank of trees. The door beeped behind her and with panic flooding her veins, she pulled it closed and dived into the tree line. She ducked behind a bush and peered through the leaves at the building.

Several seconds later, the door swung open and Peron stepped onto the landing. He cranked his head from side to side and said something over his shoulder.

How long would he stand there—waiting, watching?

A minute later, he retreated inside, but Lori didn't trust that he'd stay there. Hunching over, she traipsed through the wooded area, the twigs and pebbles biting into her feet. She circled around and came out where she was last night.

The other women must still be getting ready for dinner, as she faced an empty lawn and pool area. She ran across the grass and let herself in a side door. One of the cleaning crew looked up as she sailed past her, giving her a slight nod. She doubted the janitorial staff would report wayward guests to Reed Dufrain—but who knew?

Slightly out of breath, she shrugged out of her smock and leggings and pulled on a dress. Noticing scratches on her arms from the branches, she threw on a sweater and shoved her battered feet into a pair of flip-flops.

When she joined the others in the large, commercial-sized kitchen, she put on a smile and started dicing veggies. Nobody seemed to notice anything amiss about her appearance except for Shannon, who plucked a leaf from Lori's hair.

"The hike's not until tomorrow. Did you get an early start?"

"Just thought I heard an animal creeping around and stuck my head out there to scare him away. Peron told me there were mountain lions."

Nobody seemed to be interested in catching her out in any way and the cooking and eating of dinner passed without a hitch. But Reed and Peron had to know someone had exited that door at the end of the hallway. Security doors like that didn't just open and close on their own. They'd be on the lookout, and Peron already had her on his radar.

As Lori prepared for another hot tub session with apple cider, someone knocked on her door. "Just a second."

She rolled up her phone in her towel again and tucked it under her arm. "Come in."

Peron walked into the room, and she caught her breath. The last time she'd seen him had been when he'd been scanning the trees, looking for whoever had set off the alarm on the security door.

"Excuse me, Loretta. Reed would like to see you in his office."

Her heart slammed against her rib cage, and her hand clutched at the material of her swimsuit cover-up. "Now?"

"Yes, please. It won't take long, and then you can join the others for your swim."

"Okay." She squeezed her arm against her body, securing her towel as she followed Peron out the door and down the hallway.

He turned to the right, down a small light-filled space that contained Natasha's small office. They moved through her office to a door beyond, and Reed stood up from behind a large mahogany desk lined with computer monitors.

Lori crossed her arms over her chest and her towel, digging her fingers into her biceps. Did those monitors display images from cameras stationed throughout the center? Every move she made could've been projected back to Reed in this office.

She lifted her stiff lips into a smile. "Hello, Reed. You wanted to see me?"

"Welcome to my inner sanctum, Loretta." He tipped his head toward a comfy-looking chair on the other side of his desk. "Take a seat."

She perched on the edge of the deep armchair, afraid if she sank into it, she'd never be able to get up—or wouldn't be allowed to. She scanned the array of books behind him to avoid meeting his pale eyes.

"How are you settling in, Loretta?" He steepled his fingers and watched her above the tips.

"Fine. Great. I feel so much stronger after just a few days here. This is a wonderful program." Her hands had formed claws around the arms of the chair.

"That's nice to hear, but…" a deep furrow formed between his eyebrows "…one of our therapists believes you're closer to the edge than you think."

Lori swallowed. Where was this leading? She blinked. "Oh?"

Reed reached for a drawer and slid it open on a whisper. He pulled something from the drawer and cupped it between his hands. "We're experimenting with some vitamins here at Brighter Days that we believe are beneficial during the recovery period."

Lori licked her lips as her gaze dropped to Reed's surprisingly strong-looking fingers. "Like a weaning type of drug? I don't need that."

Reed smiled through his beard and shook the bottle of pills. "This isn't a drug at all, Loretta. It's a combination of vitamins—our own formula."

This was ridiculous. He couldn't force her to take a pill, vitamin or not, that she didn't want to take. This was a voluntary treatment center, not some court-ordered detox lockup. Peron shifted his stance to her right, moving closer to her chair.

She could take a stand right now, make a fuss, leave. What could they do at this point? They weren't going to assault her here in Reed's elegantly appointed office.

She peeled her hands from the arms of the chair and folded them in her lap. "I really don't think I need a vitamin, Reed. I feel good, strong. I'm not sure what the therapist heard from me."

Stroking his beard, Reed almost whispered, "Panic, fear, loneliness—a woman at a crossroads."

Lori locked eyes with him for a second and a shock reverberated through her body. She let her gaze wander to the bank of books behind him. If she flat-out refused, he'd probably kick her out and she'd leave with very little for her efforts. If she continued to demur and then accepted it, he'd be suspicious. If she swallowed it, she might wind up like Karenna. Even Cade might not be able to help her.

"I'm not denying I'm at a crossroads." She tilted forward slightly in her chair, resting her forearms on his desk. "What's in it?"

Reed's eyes flickered. "A combination of B, C, D,

zinc, biotin, L-carnitine and a few other natural in-gredients. We've had some amazing success with it."

Like Karenna and Diana? She wiped her hand on the thin cotton of her beach cover-up and thrust it out, palm up. "I'll give it a try. I'm committed to this process, and I want to continue on this path."

"Excellent. Of course, we can't force you to take anything here, and we wouldn't want to do that." He shook a white pill into his hand and dropped it into her palm. The light gave it a pink tint.

"All that in this little pill." Was this the same drug Summer had in powder form in her closet? Lori popped the pill into her mouth. "It's so small, I don't even need water."

Reed rubbed his hands together. "Excellent. I'll have Peron put a supply of these in your room. Take another one before you turn in tonight and another in the morning. You won't feel the effects right away—it's just a vitamin, after all—but by the end of your stay with us, you'll feel like a new woman."

"Thanks, Reed. Thank you for thinking of me." She rose from the chair. "I'm going to join the other ladies at the hot tub."

"Sweet dreams, Loretta."

She nodded to Peron and forced her steps to slow down as she left the lion's den. She sailed through Natasha's office and when she pushed through the doors that led to the patio, she shoved her finger in her mouth and scooped the pill from beneath her tongue.

She carefully tucked the damp pill into her towel and spit out the bitter residue on the ground. Reed suspected her of something, and now she'd have to watch her back like never before. But he'd given her a gift. She had one of his drugs and there would be more by her bedside tonight.

Now just might be the time to make her move and get out of here. If she didn't, she might end up one of Reed's zombies—or worse.

As she soaked in the Jacuzzi with the other women and played nice, she didn't mention Reed's special vitamin. Any one of these people could be his spy. She didn't believe for one minute either of the therapists she'd seen in group or individually had reported her *instability* to Reed. She'd barely said two words in those sessions.

She didn't trust the apple cider, either. She didn't want to eat any of the food here. He could be spiking all of it. She said her good-nights and pulled her cover-up over her wet one-piece suit. She grabbed her towel and held it in a tight roll to keep both the phone and now the pill tucked inside.

She padded to her room and closed the door, her gaze immediately traveling to her nightstand containing a bottle. Sitting on the edge of her bed, she picked it up between two fingers and opened the lid. True to his word, Reed had left her several of the pills.

She shook her phone from her towel and snapped a picture of the bottle and the pills. Then she wrapped the phone and the bottle back up and snuck outside. The women had left the hot tub and steam rose from the water and curled away into the night.

Lori ducked back onto the path through the trees and punched in Cade's number.

The first words out of his mouth made her feel warmer than the Jacuzzi. "I'm worried about you. Is everything okay?"

"I'm fine." *For now.* She ran a fingertip around the bottle cap.

"I'm here, Lori."

"I know you are, Cade, and I appreciate it, especially after I threw you for a loop the other night."

"No, I mean I'm *here*, in Topanga."

"Why? Where are you?"

"Listen, I met with your friend Trevor Jansen. He had the drug analyzed today and called you back with the results. I answered your phone. Summer had a powerful synthetic drug in the fentanyl family. He said they've been seeing it on the street in the past nine months. They don't know where it's coming from and just when they get a line on a dealer, that dealer disappears. And, get this. The dealers are primarily young women."

Lori put her hand over her mouth. "It's Reed Dufrain. If he's not manufacturing the drug somewhere, he's the one distributing it. He must be using women from Brighter Days to do his dirty work. I have the drug, Cade, right in my hot little hands."

"Why? How do you have the drug, Lori? Did you

steal it? You need to get out of there before they catch you."

"Dufrain gave it to me—to take. He called it a special vitamin."

"God, Lori. He knows you're up to something. Leave now. Take that trail and meet me at the turn-out on Topanga Canyon. I'll be waiting."

"Cade, I..." She glanced down at her cover-up, damp where it lay against her wet swimsuit. She hadn't planned on running tonight.

A twig snapping to her left sent a wave of adren-aline rushing through her body. When she heard a whisper, she cut off the call.

The recognizable voice rose, and while she wanted to run, her feet seemed rooted to the ground. "Shut up, Peron. I know she's out here. Loretta! Come out, come out, wherever you are. I have some more vi-tamins for you—and this time you're going to take them."

Chapter Eighteen

Lori dropped to the ground and crawled into a hollowed-out area between a fallen log and a bush. She dragged the gauzy cotton of her cover-up around her, tucking in the edges, and peered between the leaves.

A beam of light swung along the path, right over her hiding place, gliding across the bush. She held her breath.

Dufrain came crashing down the trail, not even attempting to be stealthy, his flowing clothes replaced by dark jeans and a hoodie. "Get out here, Loretta. I'm going to make your wildest dreams come true. You can stay high all the time and earn a ton of cash. Not a bad deal."

She clutched her hands together, digging her nails into her palms, hoping that Cade wouldn't call her back.

"Start moving, Peron. You need to find her. I have work to do. She can't stay out here all night."

Dufrain and Peron moved into her line of vision, and her muscles ached with the tension of keeping still.

Peron scrabbled in the dirt and leaves, and then bent over and yanked something. A lid? A manhole in the forest? He cleared a path and Dufrain stepped to the edge of the clearing.

"Come back for me in two hours."

Dufrain descended into the ground, as Lori clasped both hands over her mouth. Where the hell was he going? Or maybe he was descending into hell, where he belonged.

When he disappeared, Peron covered the space with the leaves and twigs and turned to peer into the darkness. Would he continue looking for her as Dufrain ordered?

He finally moved toward the light and warmth of the center. Dufrain obviously didn't think she was too much of a threat if he'd abandoned his search for her. He probably thought she had no way out, no way of contacting anyone. He hadn't been watching her as closely as she thought he was.

She waited another ten minutes. She had no hope of following Dufrain into his underground bunker— and she didn't want to do it alone.

She didn't have to. She had Cade.

CADE SAT IN his car tapping the phone against the steering wheel. If Lori didn't show up soon, he'd dive in there and look for her. She'd cut off the call so abruptly, he figured she was in trouble but was hoping for a call back.

As he snatched the keys from the ignition and grabbed the door handle, a vision appeared out the window—a vision in a short white dress, bare legs and sandals.

He shot out of the car and engulfed her in a hug. "Thank God you're out of there. Did you get the pills?"

The pills clattered as she shook a bottle. "I have them, but we have to go back."

"You just escaped. You're not going back in there."

"Cade, Dufrain has an underground bunker. I saw him go into it. Summer might be there. Courtney. We have to follow him."

His head jerked up. "You think he's keeping them somewhere?"

"It's a possibility. He's drugging women with this synthetic concoction, turning them into zombies and then forcing them to sell this stuff on the street. When things get too hot—it's like Trevor told you— he yanks them off the street and replaces them with new dealers so that the product doesn't get traced back to him." She grabbed his shirt. "When I was talking to one of his drugged-out disciples, she told me the other women were *below*. I didn't know what she meant at the time, but I do now. We have to go back. I can show you where it is. Dufrain is coming back up in two hours. We can surprise him."

"We can't do this alone, Lori, even with your gun in my backpack. We have to call the police."

"And tell them what? There are women on drugs in a drug treatment center and the director has an underground bunker? They can't move in on that information. They'll even have to test the pills I give them. If I've learned anything working with the LAPD, it's that they have a process they need to follow, or the DA will throw out the whole case. They have to collect evidence and get a judge to sign off on a search warrant. If they don't, nothing they find in an illegal search is worth anything. We started this on our own, and we're gonna have to finish it on our own."

"You're right. We can't wait any longer. I brought a backpack just in case I had to go in and rescue you from that place." He reached behind him for the car door. "Let me get that. Do you want a sweatshirt? Why are you wearing a bathing suit under that thing?"

"It's a long story. I'll take the sweatshirt…and the gun."

"I'm not going to sit here and have an argument with you about who handles a gun better, but since it's yours, you take it. If Dufrain has Summer down there, I'm not going to need a gun to take care of him." He hoisted the backpack over his shoulders and they moved down the road to the trailhead.

They followed Cade's flashlight along the same path they'd gone a few days before until Lori held out an arm to stop him. "This is where we veer to the left. We need to be on the lookout for Peron. He's Dufrain's henchman."

Animals scurried out of their way as they plowed through the underbrush. Cade stalled when he saw the lights from the center. "Do you think he has cameras out here?"

Lori answered, "I'm not sure, but it's not like he has a security team patrolling the place. I wouldn't think he'd want his comings and goings recorded for posterity, either."

Cade dropped back as Lori led the way to an area that looked as if it had been disturbed already tonight. "It's here. There must be some kind of lever or something."

He dropped to his knees beside her, and together they pushed aside the natural debris of the forest, which formed a thin layer over a hard, square cover with a heavy ring on it.

"The handle." Lori lifted it. "If Peron could pull this open alone, you shouldn't have any trouble."

From a crouching position, Cade grasped the ring with both hands and braced his feet against the ground. One hard yank cracked the doorway, and he lifted it wide enough for Lori to shimmy through the gap.

She called up, "There are steps."

Cade held the lid open until he slid through, and then he lowered it into place. He immediately covered his nose against the sickly, sweet smell that permeated the air. He gagged. "What is that?"

"I have no idea." Lori pulled the neck of her sweatshirt over her mouth and nose.

"Keep that sweatshirt in place." Cade tugged a ski mask from his backpack and covered the lower half of his face. He then pulled his phone from his pocket and in a muffled voice said, "I'm sharing my location with Jansen for as long as I can. I'm sure service will be cut off soon."

They descended until they reached a flat, dirt surface. Cade hopped off the last step, cocking his head. He whispered, "Do you hear that?"

"Metal scraping against metal?" Lori pulled out her gun, and Cade gripped a short club in his hand and killed his flashlight. They didn't need to announce their arrival.

Hugging the damp walls, they crept down the passage until the clinking and clanking sound grew louder and the smell more noxious. They rounded a bend and froze as a clearing opened in front of them.

A small underground lab appeared like some kind of drug dealer's mirage. What made the scene more surreal were the lab workers in white hazmat suits moving from station to station sliding along chains suspended from the ceiling and connected to belts around their waists.

Dufrain had enslaved these people to manufacture his drugs. Were these all women? Dufrain's clients? Summer?

Cade stiffened, and Lori placed a hand on his arm. One of the suited-up workers had to be Dufrain himself. Lori had seen him come down here.

Lori took a few steps back and put her mouth close to his ear. "We can't stay here. The fumes are going to overwhelm us."

"We can't leave them here. What if one of those automatons is Summer? I can't abandon her, Lori. What made Dufrain think he could do this to Summer? He must've believed she was utterly alone. *She* must've believed that."

"I understand, Cade. Really, I do, but if we don't get into a hazmat suit and join the fun or get out of here, we're going to pass out."

He didn't know if it was Lori's suggestion or if the chemicals really were affecting him, but Cade felt a wave of nausea course through him. "Okay, but we get Jansen, and the whole sheriff's department to swarm this place once we're out. I don't care what it takes. I'll report a dead body down here if I have to."

She held up the cell phone he'd returned to her. "Once they see a picture of this, we won't need a dead body."

She ducked around the corner once more and then seconds later joined him again, stuffing the phone in her pocket. "Let's go."

They reached the stairs and Cade stepped aside. "You first."

"If we're not waiting for Peron to show up, you'd better go first. I'm not sure I can lift that lid."

He swung himself onto the ladder and said, "Stay close."

About halfway to the top, Lori yelped behind him. He twisted around to see someone coming up the step behind her. Cade roared. "Move!"

He took another step but almost missed it when Lori cried out, "He's got my ankle."

"Where's your gun?"

"In my pocket. Go, Cade. Get help, or we'll both die here."

A voice boomed below Lori. "I'm not going to kill you, Loretta. You're coming to work for me."

A white, hot anger pounded through Cade and he descended another step.

Dufrain, his beard wildly sticking out from a bandanna around the lower half of his face, had a hand wrapped around one of Lori's ankles. "In fact, I could use both of you in my stable."

Lori looked up at Cade with her big brown eyes set in a determined glare. "Get out, Cade. You can come back for this piece of garbage."

Dufrain clicked his tongue. "I'm one step ahead of you, junkie scum. When I spotted you in here, I radioed ahead to Peron. He and another one of my orderlies will be waiting on the other side of the doorway with some weapons—and theirs will be in their hand, not uselessly stuck in their pockets."

Lori kicked out with her other foot but Dufrain ducked the blow.

"In fact, your training is going to start right now,

Loretta." He wrapped his other arm around the ladder and secured Lori's leg with that hand and then reached into his pocket, emerging with a needle. "The pill I gave you earlier, which you probably didn't even swallow, was just a starter dose. The drug in this syringe will make you mine in a matter of seconds."

With both of Dufrain's hands occupied, Cade took his chance. He lowered himself, coiled his leg and stomped on Dufrain's head.

Dufrain gasped, and he released his hold on Lori to claw for one of the rungs.

Lori kicked the hand holding the needle and Dufrain flailed for a second or two before plunging backward off the ladder with a scream.

Chapter Nineteen

Lori leaned against the ladder, breathing hard, her head swimming. "Cade, we have to get out of here. I'm going to pass out. If Peron is on the other side, you can use my gun on him."

"Can you hold on to my leg? I'll get you out."

As she circled her fingers around Cade's ankle, a square opened above them, and bright light flooded the area.

"Stop right there. Don't make another move. LAPD."

Lori had never been happier to hear that announcement. "Trevor? It's Lori and Cade, and we just found you a drug lab."

"That's what it smells like. Get out of there before you succumb to the fumes."

As Cade clambered out, he said, "There are people in chains down there. We have to get them out."

Trevor's jaw dropped. "Are you telling me he's forcing people to work for him?"

Cade turned around to help Lori out of the hole in the ground, and she collapsed on the dirt, gulping in the fresh air. When Lori's head rolled to the side, she saw Peron and another man she hadn't seen before, handcuffed and sitting by a tree.

"Yeah, he has them chained up to some apparatus so that they can move about, and one of those people might be my sister. I'm going back down with you."

"Stay here. A few of the guys went down already. They'll bring everyone out."

A head popped up from the entrance to the bunker. "Jansen, you're not gonna believe what's been going on down here."

"I just heard. Bring those people up. I have an ambulance on the way, and I'll call for more. Lori said there are women inside the center in distress, and we need to question everyone who worked there to find out if and how they were involved in Dufrain's sick business. Do you have Reed Dufrain in custody?"

The other cop shrugged. "Easy. He was out cold when we found him."

"The fumes?"

Cade said, "Ah, that would be us. He came after Lori, and I kicked him down the ladder. Too bad he's still alive."

Trevor narrowed his eyes. "No, that's a good thing for you, Larson."

Minutes later, Lori watched, as if in a dream, woman after woman emerging from the bunker in a hazmat suit, pulling the headpiece off and staggering toward an officer or sinking to the ground. How Trevor had gotten all these cops from the LA

County Sheriff's Department to show up, she didn't know, but they were needed.

As a tall woman peeled off her headgear and shook out her blond hair, Cade shouted and bounded to his feet. He grabbed his sister and pulled her into a hug, hazmat suit and all.

Lori rested her head back on the ground, a smile spreading across her face.

Epilogue

A few days after the raid, Lori had invited Summer and Cade to her house to compare notes.

Summer scooped her hair back from her face and curled one leg beneath her. "Do you think Reed knew who you were when you went to Brighter Days?"

Lori eyed Cade on his phone, pacing the back patio. "He didn't know, or he never would've allowed me to go there."

"But what about your slashed tires and…and Trey Ferrar's murder?" Summer cupped a mug of tea in her hands, her color back in her cheeks and a sheen creeping back into her blond tresses.

"Reed's guys weren't following me. They were watching your place, saw my car there and slashed the tires as a warning. Same with Trey. He started calling Brighter Days when Courtney went missing, as she'd done a stint there a few months earlier. He didn't like the answers they were giving him." Lori gave an involuntary shiver. "Reed was having Trey followed. They scared him off enough that he didn't mention it to the police but when Cade and I approached him, he was ready to talk."

"So, they took their opportunity when Trey went to the bar." Summer sniffed and rubbed her nose with the back of her hand. "Courtney's all messed up about that."

"I'm sure she is." Lori watched Cade waving one arm in the air. If that was a work call, something must need his attention. "You and Courtney weren't friends before?"

"We met after becoming Reed's lackeys."

"And you two and the other woman, Chelsea, all cleverly decided to leave your fingerprints at each other's places to send a message to the cops, linking you all together."

"We messed up our places, also. We figured people would be looking for us once Reed took us. I knew Cade was expecting me, so I was sure he'd find my disappearance suspicious. We just didn't know how else to get a message out. Reed and his minions controlled our actions, supplied us with pink China Girl and made us sell it for him." She held her hands. "I never would've sold that stuff for him, but he got us hooked. When things got too hot on the street, he sent his henchmen to grab us and imprison us in the drug bunker. We didn't want to disappear without a trace so we left our prints…and you did figure it out."

"It wasn't quite enough for the police though."

Summer's gaze wandered to the patio. "I knew it would be enough for Cade. I knew he wouldn't let me down. He never lets anyone down—not even you, Lori. If he'd known about the baby, he would've stayed."

"I know that."

Cade opened the sliding door and stepped into the kitchen, wrinkling his nose at their cups. "Hot tea? The sun's starting to come out, you know."

"Finally." Summer stretched her legs out like a cat, and then crossed them. "What was that phone call all about? You weren't talking to Mom and Dad, were you?"

"Not yet, but we'll have to tell them, and Sarah, too." He clamped a hand on his sister's shoulder. "Don't worry. They're not going to blame you, Summer. It's not your fault."

"If I hadn't gone back on the drugs, I never would've had to check myself in to Brighter Days. Reed never would've targeted me to become one of his drug pushers."

"How are the other women?" Lori pressed a hand over her heart. "How are Karenna and Diana? I never even saw Diana there."

"Reed already had Diana on the street selling. He'd groom us to sell, send us back out into the city and if anyone started sniffing around, he'd drag us to the drug lab to cook. That way, he had a rotating group of pushers. We never escaped because he had us addicted and he threatened to turn us in—or worse. I don't think he would've hesitated to kill any one of us."

"And the rest?"

"We're all recovering. Some are in worse shape than others, but one of the therapists at Brighter Days is forming a recovery-support group."

Cade growled. "You'd trust someone from that place?"

"Hannah felt terrible that she was part of Brighter Days and that Reed was committing those atrocities, literally right beneath her. She knew nothing about it. Most of the women knew nothing about it. He operated a legit treatment center in addition to his drug trade. The police have already questioned and exonerated Hannah—Natasha, too, although she suspected something wasn't right. Anyway, Hannah reached out to all of us, and is offering her services for free."

"And you?" Lori took Summer's pale hand. "Are you okay now?"

"I'm not gonna lie. That China Girl that we were manufacturing was some primo stuff—smooth high and completely addictive. My doc has me on some tranquilizers to ease the transition, but I'm going to be okay under his supervision and I'm going back to NA. That program works for me." She squeezed Lori's hand and patted her brother's still resting on her shoulder. "I swear."

Lori swirled her tea in the bottom of her cup. "What was that phone call out there? You're not doing any more digging around in our daughter's life, are you?"

"That's done. I have the PI's report and I can share it with you when you're ready, but it's nothing you don't already know. She's in a good home with loving parents, she adores her little brother, she does well in school and she's well-adjusted. She's living the life you gave her, the one you made possible by your unselfish act."

A pool of tears formed in Lori's eyes. "Thanks for that...and your forgiveness."

Shaking her head, Summer pushed back from her chair. "You two were always made for each other. Have you figured that out yet?"

Lori's eyes met Cade's, and his lips twisted up on one side. "I think I'm figuring it out."

"I think I'm going to leave you two to come to your senses. I'm having lunch with Courtney today. She's having a tough time with Trey's death, and I'm going to be there for her."

When Summer left the house, Lori turned to Cade. "When are you going back to New York? My suspension is up, and I'm returning to work tomorrow. No more Nancy Drew. I'm also on probation for my latest stunt, so I have to watch myself."

"I'm leaving later in the week, but you should visit me before I move."

Lori's heart jumped. "You're leaving New York?"

"I've got a perfectly good house in Malibu—if you've figured out the same thing I've figured out."

Curling her arms around Cade's neck, she said, "I think I knew it all along."

"Great. Let's get going, or we'll miss it."

"Miss what?" She flattened her hands against his chest.

"Visiting hours."

"At the correctional institution? You're coming with me to visit Danny?"

"You helped me find my sister, and now I'm going to help you find your brother."

Cade wouldn't give her any more information than that, not even on the long drive out to Tehachapi. He joined her in the visiting room and had a brief conversation with Danny before leaving them together.

Danny smiled when he left. "The two of you are getting back together? You and the rich kid."

"As soon as he moves back here from New York, we're going to see how it goes."

"You told him about the kid?"

"I did. He forgives me."

"People need forgiveness." Danny ran a tattooed hand across his buzz cut. "Cade's a good guy, always was. Cares about you."

"I know that." She tilted her head. "What is it, Danny?"

"Yeah, I have something to tell you, Lori."

Twenty minutes later Lori walked into the sunshine, blinking. Cade rose from the bench beneath the looming oak and wrapped his arms around her. "Did he tell you?"

She pressed her wet face against Cade's chest.

"He told me he killed Elena—a fit of passion, he said. D-did you ask him to tell me?"

"I did. I told him he needed to release you, release you from that fantasy you wove around him. How do you feel?"

"Disappointed. Deflated, in a way. Free."

"Did you tell him you forgave him?"

"It's not for me to forgive him, is it? That's for Elena's family to work out."

"You need to forgive him for holding you captive all this time, for lying to you, for perpetuating a fraud against you."

She pulled away from Cade and held his hands. "I forgave him for that. I'm visiting him in a few weeks. I won't abandon him, even though there's a part of him that's a monster. I still need time to reconcile that piece of him with the sweet, gentle Danny I know. I suppose I should tell Mom and the rest of the family."

He cupped her face with one hand. "Your mother knows. They've all known for years."

"You're right." She wiped the back of her hand across her damp cheek. "Was this a condition of your moving back here? Of seeing me again?"

"My love for you has no conditions, but I wanted you to move on from the lie you were telling yourself." He stroked the side of her face with his thumb. "Can you do that now?"

"I think I'm moving away from a lot of lies." She

captured his hand and kissed his palm. "As long as I have you by my side, I think I can do anything."

"Then you can do anything, Loretta Maria Del Valle, because I'm not going anywhere."

And as he held her there outside the prison walls, she felt free to love him with all her heart.

* * * * *

Look for the next book in Carol Ericson's The Lost Girls series, Lakeside Mystery, *on sale next month, only from Harlequin Intrigue!*

His hands cupped her face. She blinked up at him.

"They buried me," she said, fighting the emotion
trying to take over at the thought of never seeing him
again.

Anger flashed in his blue eyes, and his jaw muscles
clenched. "They better never touch you again. We can
make an excuse to get you out of here. Say one of your
family members is sick and you had to go."

"They'll see it as weakness," she reminded him. "It'll
hurt the case."

He thumbed a loose tendril of hair off her face.

"I don't care, Ree," he said with an overwhelming
intensity that became its own physical presence. "I can't
lose you."

Those words hit her with the force of a tsunami.

HIEXP0622

Neither of them could predict what would happen next. Neither could guarantee this case wouldn't go south. Neither could guarantee they would both walk away in one piece.

"Let's take ourselves off the case together," she said, knowing full well he wouldn't take her up on the offer but suggesting it anyway.

Quint didn't respond. When she pulled back and looked into his eyes, she understood why. A storm brewed behind those sapphire-blues, crystalizing them, sending fiery streaks to contrast against the whites. Those babies were the equivalent of a raging wildfire that would be impossible to put out or contain. People said eyes were the window to the soul. In Quint's case, they seemed the window to his heart.

He pressed his forehead against hers and took in an audible breath. When he exhaled, it was like he was releasing all his pent-up frustration and fear. In that moment, she understood the gravity of what he'd been going through while she'd been gone. Kidnapped. For all he knew, left for dead.

So she didn't speak, either. Instead, she leaned into their connection, a connection that tethered them as an electrical current ran through her to him and back. For a split second, it was impossible to determine where he ended and she began.

Don't miss
Mission Honeymoon *by Barb Han,*
available August 2022 wherever
Harlequin Intrigue books and ebooks are sold.

Harlequin.com